To Teresa and Norma
with love
Lucia
1992

BORDER CROSSING

BORDER CROSSING
a novel
by
Lisa Herman

MOSAIC PRESS
Oakville-New York-London

CANADIAN CATALOGUING IN PUBLICATION DATA

Herman, Lisa
    Border crossing

ISBN 0-88962-523-9 (bound)   0-88962-524-7 (pbk.)

I. Title

PS8565.E75B6 1992   C813'.54   C92-094970-3
PR9199.3.H37B6 1992

No part of this book may be reproduced or transmitted in any form, by any means, electronic or mechanical, including photocopying and recording information storage and retrieval systems, without permission in writing from the publisher, except by a reviewer who may quote brief passages in a review.

Published by MOSAIC PRESS, P.O. Box 1032, Oakville, Ontario, L6J 5E9, Canada. Offices and warehouse at 1252 Speers Road, Unit #1 &2, Oakville, Ontario, L6L 5N9, Canada.

Mosaic Press acknowledges the assistance of the Canada Council and the Ontario Arts Council in support of its publishing programme.

Copyright © Lisa Herman, 1992
Design by Patty Gallinger
Typeset by Jackie Ernst
Printed and bound in Canada.

ISBN   0-88962-523-9 HC   0-88962-524-7 PB

MOSAIC PRESS:
In Canada:
    MOSAIC PRESS, 1252 Speers Road, Units #1&2, Oakville, Ontario, L6L 5N9, P.O. Box 1032, Oakville, Ontario, L6J 5E9, Canada.
In the United States:
  National Book Network, Inc., 4720-A Boston Way, Lanham, M.D., 20706, U.S.A.
In the U.K.:
    John Calder (Publishers) Ltd., 9-15 Neal Street, London, WC2 H9TU, England

*In memory
Chaim, Eliyah, Tzabri*

Chapter 1

There are beaches on the Sinai peninsula on the eastern coast of Egypt that are still as pure as when they were created. Only white sand, blue sea and the occasional date palm cohabit here. The area is protected from the inland by a desert and then by the mountain range where God gave the world the Ten Commandments. Here, divers frequent the coral reefs, blue-jeaned tourists discover paradise, and Israelis, since the 1967 War and access rights, sometimes seek peace.

Arlene, Daniel and Mussa are lying on a beach called Ras Burka. Mussa, the Palestinian, is asleep and dreaming about a French film. Daniel, the Jew, traces criss-crossed shapes in the sand. Arlene, the American, stares out at the water. All three are Israeli tourists.

"I'm glad you talked me into coming," says Arlene.

Daniel smiles into the sand.

"Okay. So I was a tough case."

Daniel still doesn't respond.

"But I am trying to thank you, Daniel."

He outlines a fortress and then proceeds to cover it with hatch marks. As if I don't see her happiness, he thinks. It's been months since I've seen her eyes clear like this, her face relaxed, her hands quiet by her sides. She's a beautiful woman when she has enough space around her.

Mussa turns onto his side and grumbles in his sleep.

"You must be patient with him, Arlene," says Daniel. "He gets hurt easily."

"And hurts back too," she answers.

Daniel sighs. I will lie between them, he thinks. The American and the Arab. And give them time to know each other.

Mussa wakes up. Disoriented, he first feels the terrycloth towel beneath him and then Daniel by his side.

"You guys missed a terrific battle," he invents. "We had you Jews at our mercy - begging for your lives."

"Then you ran out of ammunition, your tanks broke down and the air cover got lost," says Daniel. "So we rounded all of you up and sent you to high school."

How can they joke about the conflict? thinks Arlene. And then, as usual, turns her criticism on herself. And who am I to judge? As far as Mussa's concerned, I'm a body with no mind. And to Daniel I'm a hopelessly out-of-touch idealist. So what am I doing here in this place with two people who don't even know I exist?

"I'm going for a swim."

The two men watch her receding body - black shoulder-length hair, brown back crossed by a thin green bikini strap and a tiny, green bikini bottom that shows a hint of buttocks melting into long, brown legs.

"She's pretty," says Mussa.

"She thinks you don't like her. You must try and be nicer, Mussa. That way you'll get to know her."

Mussa sits up, brushing the sand off the curls of dark hair on his chest. "I'm taking this vacation as it comes. We're all of us crazy coming down to the Sinai together. You're the craziest, though."

Daniel now draws a giant chicken in the sand and then uses a pebble to add his delicate criss-crosses. Yes, I am the craziest. And I am drowning in fear. But you will not know how deep I am sinking, Mussa. And the three of us will have our vacation. And you will not let me fall into the abyss. And I'll rest and return to work and function until I fall apart again.

The stretch of beach on the Red Sea is deserted except for the two dark bodies on bright towels. The woman wades into the water. Behind the men a plastic awning and a palm tree cast shade. Nearby there is a green canvas tent and a Volkswagen. The van's black sides glisten with freckles of wind-draped sand. Daniel drops the pebble and reaches into his day-pack to pull out a cellophane package and some rolling papers. He rolls, smokes and then passes the joint to his friend.

"She has three kids, you know," says Daniel. "Their father is at home with them. He's Israeli born."

Mussa chuckles. "I'm sure he's delighted that the mother of his children is spending her vacation with two male friends, one a maniac and the other an Arab."

"Well, I'm not sure he knows you're here," says Daniel.

Arlene faces the sea, standing deep enough so the water just covers her breasts. If I were to sail from here I would reach the Indian Ocean, she thinks. But I'd probably get shot first. And if Mussa were to sail they would shoot him too. From a distance no one would know who was an Arab and who was a Jew.

Arlene often contemplates the limits as to how far she can go. To manage this on the edge of an ocean is a feat of some distinction, but Arlene is used to making walls and corners in places where others would have openings. She is attempting to experience her present situation as non-sexual, and this is a difficult task. If she needs reinforcement in her thinking, she decides she'll drive to the nearest telephone and call her children.

Wife and mother of three, what am I doing here? I can feel them watching and they too want to know why I'm with them. They would be more comfortable by themselves. Relaxed. But Daniel seemed so anxious for me to come.

She remembers their lunch in the Tel Aviv café when Daniel convinced her to take this vacation with him. He almost pleaded, so that she ended up asking him why it was so important.

"Forget it," he answered.

But she didn't believe that.

"Okay, Arlene. I'm in one of those bad times. When I don't see very far ahead. When I don't know why I bother to go on. It's too damn hard to get up in the morning and too easy to fall into bed at night. I'm smoking too much, listening to Pink Floyd and forgetting to eat. I've told you how angry they are at the office, and it was you who suggested I take a week off."

"But why with me?"

"I can't be alone and I can't be with idiots. That leaves you and Mussa. And aside from that, you're as stressed out from life here as I am."

She turns off the replay of the conversation.

On the beach Daniel and Mussa are stoned. Mussa has done most of their all-night drive from Tel Aviv and is tired. His nap has left him irritable. He would like to go for a swim but Arlene's presence in the water inhibits him.

She is Daniel's friend, he tells himself. The American. The one with the lovely body and three children and a husband.

This trip was a last-minute decision for Mussa, as are all his social arrangements. At home, Michal, his Jewish girlfriend, had gone to bed early and Mussa lay awake beside her, waiting to hear Daniel in the van outside before making up his mind. The sound of the horn below disturbed Michal in her sleep and she hugged him closer. Mussa felt restrained, got out of bed, lit the desk lamp, wrote a note and threw a few things in a shopping bag.

In the passenger seat was Arlene. He had forgotten Daniel told him she was part of the plan. He got in the back. Later Mussa took the wheel and while the other two dozed, he drove down the long straight road through the desert moonscape.

Mussa knows that he'll eventually speak to Arlene. The thought is comfortable for the moment. He pulls himself to his feet.

"You coming?"

Daniel shakes his head. Surrounded by his squared-off shapes he lies on his back, arms crossed behind brown-blond head. Without opening his eyes he can watch his friend's ritual of gradual entrance. Daniel and Mussa have spent much time together on the beach in Tel Aviv and Mussa's immersion into the ocean is always the same. First he stands with the water lapping at his toes, gazing into the distance and pretending not to notice the encroachment. Then he moves to knee depth, then on, lifting himself slightly from the hips to keep the water from his penis. Delicately his fingers trace water and then face and repeat the gestures. Last of all, he yells and dives into the ocean, volume significantly decreasing if the beach is crowded. Surfacing, he shakes his black curls ferociously, ready to dive again.

Daniel is so surprised to hear only a mild cry before the splash that he opens his eyes to see if other people have arrived.

It is difficult for Daniel to understand the tension between Arlene and Mussa. He sees other people's lives unfolding more simply than his own. And so he is often caught not prepared for their actions.

When his sister divorced her husband after ten years of marriage, she laughed at Daniel's apparent shock.

"Where've you been? Avi and I haven't looked each other in the eye for over a year. Mom keeps putting us on opposite sides of her table, trying to get us to see each other."

Daniel hadn't noticed. He had only been aware that his mother's concern was less focussed on him and he had enjoyed that.

Arlene has begun to swim and Mussa moves in the opposite direction. Daniel watches their bodies draw apart until they both disappear from view. I have delivered my friends to the sea, he thinks, and imbedded in the sand, I provide the anchor between them. If the world stops at this moment, we can die in perfect balance.

Their crossing into Egypt happened at sunrise, after a quick breakfast in the town of Eilat, on the Israeli side of the Red Sea. The soldiers paid little attention to the threesome. The border post was not yet taken seriously. The Sinai and its beaches having recently been returned in exchange for peace, the young men still thought of the other side as theirs.

However, for the three citizens, a peaceful land entry into another political entity was an exciting novelty.

On Egyptian soil Mussa spoke to the inspector in Arabic, and Daniel smiled as he watched himself become a minority - the one handicapped by language and religion, dependent on a friend to smooth things over.

So this is what it is to be a non-military Jew abroad, he thought. The way the Jews have been for thousands of years. Daniel, like most Israelis, had been taught from childhood to pity his wandering brethren.

The Egyptian inspector had called Mussa "brother" and wished him and his companions well. He then smiled at Daniel and Arlene and welcomed them in English. Arlene travelled using her Israeli passport which she shared with her children. The inspector smiled at the pictures of her two little girls and baby boy and then pointed to himself, holding up six fingers. He gave the van only a perfunctory search.

"Those pictures of your kids worked well," said Daniel as they pulled onto the road. "Kept his mind at ease. Didn't look very hard and didn't find the stuff."

"Why didn't you tell me?" Arlene had been furious. "Are you guys crazy crossing into the Sinai with dope? Do you know how many years we could get for that?"

"Arlene, two weeks of vacation with no stuff to smoke is not my idea of a vacation," answered Daniel.

She had crossed her arms and stared ahead at the road which was now bleached in sunlight. The sea peeked between sand dunes to their left and mountains rose to the right.

"Simple people like the guard don't realize that children can be politically conscious," added Mussa. He was amused at the incident. "Kids are usually ignored and that's what makes them such excellent recruits for front-line fighting."

Daniel had warned him, "No politics, my friend. You promised." But sitting in the front seat next to Mussa, Arlene had wanted to talk to him, to understand what he meant, to know what he remembered.

"Do you have kids?" she asked.

But Mussa didn't answer.

In America Arlene never thought about Arabs living inside Israel. She perceived them only as a people surrounding her own. She had come to spend time in a Jewish state and study at the Hebrew University in Jerusalem. There she met her Israeli husband and moved to Tel Aviv. Arabs were still not part of her circle. But as the Arab population in Israel grew more vocal, everyone became conscious of their existence. Arlene was sympathetic to their grievances but not personally involved. Occasionally an Arab intellectual appeared at someone's party but Arlene felt too intimidated to talk.

When they reached the small green sign "Ras Burka," Daniel said, "This is our beach. Pull off here, Mussa."

"What does the name mean, Mussa?" Arlene asked, in another attempt at communication.

"Ras Burka is Arabic for Shining Head."

A road descended from the highway to the beach. It led past a corrugated metal shack and a flagpole with a tattered Egyptian flag, which were soon hidden by a huge sand dune shimmering in the sunlight. The cobalt sea lay before them. The small white beach with its single date palm was deserted. Mussa stopped the van so they could memorize the view.

"Ido at the office was right," said Daniel. "We have the place all to ourselves. That's Hakkal in Saudi Arabia across the water, and just to the northwest you can see the town of Aqaba in Jordan."

They drove down to the sand.

The two men set up Daniel's tent. Arlene arranged her four-poled awning, extending the shade of the palm tree, and placed her cooler beneath it. Then in the van where she would sleep, she changed into her bathing suit, pulled a towel around her and joined Daniel and Mussa in the sun.

"I hadn't pictured this place as so isolated, with no other people around. Quite a difference from the crowded Israeli beaches," she says, wiping mango juice from her chin.

They are eating lunch after Arlene and Mussa's swim, enjoying fresh vegetables, fruit, bread and cheese before having to turn to canned things.

This emptiness is hard for me, Arlene thinks. I'm not sure how to fill it. No one is demanding my attention. And I already miss Yossi and the kids.

The men are engrossed in their food.

"If you guys don't want me to freak out, you're going to have to talk more. There's a limit to the duration of a silence field I can function in."

The men nod.

"Daniel?"

"Don't worry." Daniel reaches over and rubs her head. "He's shy."

Arlene snorts a laugh.

"Why are you laughing?" Mussa is defensive.

"You know why."

"Why?"

Their eyes meet and she challenges him, thinking of how he undresses her in his mind. Embarrassed, they look at the sand.

Now Daniel laughs and Mussa glares at him, then asks, "Why must Americans talk so much?"

Arlene answers, "Maybe we're interested in what we have to say to each other."

Daniel brings the plastic water container from the van. It's heavy and his back aches. He stumbles and Mussa rushes to take the container from him.

"You know you shouldn't be carrying anything."

Arlene's face lights up at Mussa's concern. He turns to her.

"You asked me if I have children. I have two daughters in my village in the north."

Arlene is perplexed as to why he has chosen to tell her.

But he has felt the moment of shared caring for Daniel. "You mustn't underestimate me. You Americans do that when you run up against something different from yourselves."

"What does that mean?"

"I have my own inner timetable. You'll have to devote some time to learning it."

She smiles.

This is how I wanted it to be, thinks Daniel. Life flowing in and out of each other's head. He rolls a joint for Mussa and himself and they move their towels under the awning.

Arlene stretches out in the noontime sun and reads John LeCarre's *The Little Drummer Girl*, which her mother sent her from the States. She glances at Daniel to see if he will tease her. He knows her addiction to paperbacks and has already complained about the couple of books she brought with her. But Arlene cannot function well unless a never-before-read book is easily available. As a child, having finished a book and no chance for a few hours to pick up a new one, she would throw tantrums - uncontrollable emotional states that left her parents bewildered. Sometimes there were even physical manifestations - shaking and shortness of breath.

Arlene's husband and Daniel find common ground in their amused tolerance for her compulsion.

Mussa smokes and watches Arlene. Shit, why did Daniel bring her?

Women, and not the dream of Palestine, are Mussa's obsession. In pursuit of a female, he is at least clear in his objective. The goal of destroying the State of Israel is not so simple. Though in theory he believes the State should not exist - that it was founded by a guilt-ridden western world to compensate for its own mistakes towards the Jews - Mussa has always felt separated from his people's struggle, tainted by growing up inside the westernized Jewish State. He has learned some Yiddish through forbidden eavesdropping on his father's Jewish clients. His friends are both Arabs and Jews and he feels more at home debating issues in the cafés of Tel Aviv than on his knees facing Mecca.

Mussa has accepted that he could never become a devout Muslim living in a Palestinian state. That he is awkwardly comfortable with his present fringe status in the Jewish "homeland." This self-knowledge leads him to depression, and he lies on the sand once again aware of the contradiction and feeling his erection grow.

My miserable body is being lit on fire by this symbol of American imperialism in the Middle East, he chides himself, and takes another drag.

"Did I tell you the kids wanted to come with us?" Arlene calls to Daniel.

In Tel Aviv her husband's parents and Daniel's parents are acquainted. He met her as Yossi's wife; and sometimes Daniel imagines he is married to Arlene, that her children are his. He often visits their home as "Uncle Daniel" and so can easily place himself in scenes there. But he is grateful she is married. If she were not securely tied to another, he would have had to stay distant.

With the exception of Arlene, Daniel has never allowed any relationship but one of casual sex with a woman. Anyone who managed to evoke emotion in him was abandoned. It was a conscious decision not to "burden" another with his problems. But Arlene sought him out, managed to get him to talk to her, and quietly insinuated herself into being his first woman friend.

The exhaustion from the night's drive and the tension of being together catch up with them and they drift off.

Arlene wakes with a sunburn, the ultra-violet rays having worked through her Coppertone. She is alone on the beach.

I guess they'll be back, she thinks. She goes to the Volkswagen and splashes vinegar over her skin to cool down, then changes into loose pants and shirt. The angle of the sun has changed and she repositions the awning poles. The solitude disturbs her.

I don't know who I am by myself. I stop existing. I wish I were home where I belong.

Daniel and Mussa have gone for a walk beyond their beach. Daniel is worried that Mussa regrets coming, that he is angry at him.

The two met at a party and became linked through shared black humour at the crazed world around them. Their times together are spent criticizing each other, relieving their tension and despair. Neither one is used to the present tranquility around them.

"Will Michal still be there when you get back?" asks Daniel. "She blames me for dragging you here. She's always hated me."

"Daniel, you're paranoid. She doesn't hate you. And she's not leaving me. That woman is loyal. Through thick and thin. And that's how she holds me. Otherwise, I probably would have been out of there a long time ago. She loves me."

"Because she's a Jew who puts up with you just like a good Arab woman? That's love?"

"Yes."

"And do you love her?"

"Of course I do." Mussa smiles, a wide mischievous grin with shy downcast eyes. "Women are different, Daniel. They know how to love better than we do."

"I've comforted more than one of your discarded ones. Most of them good Jewish girls too. What's your secret?"

Mussa throws a pebble into the ocean, watching it arc out and sink. "Are you asking my advice, Daniel? You want to know how to interest more women? Arab, Jewish or your *goyishe* tourist - if you want lovers, just don't tell them how fucked up you are. Leave them some fantasies. Let them do the talking."

"They do talk to me, Mussa. And they pour their hearts out about broken love affairs with people like you."

"And Arlene?"

"We're friends. I told you that. I'm a friend of the whole family. I'm no threat. Her husband knows that and Arlene knows it and her kids know it. Uncle Daniel."

"And what about me?"

"What about you?"

"Who am I to Arlene?"

"You are my friend, Mussa. You are someone I trust and so she must learn to trust you too. I know we usually think in terms of fucking, but this woman and you will be friends."

"Give me a break, Daniel."

Daniel laughs. "Get to know her, that's all."

"Are you in love, Daniel?"

"You know that's not in my bag of tricks."

Maybe I can get a bus out of here tomorrow, thinks Mussa. That is the best thing I can do for Daniel - leave him alone with his American woman. Something will either happen between them or not. I don't belong here with these two Jews in this Arab country that isn't my own. They're bona fide tourists, while I'm some kind of voyeur. Perhaps if Daniel and I were alone it might have been all right. We would have got stoned and laughed. I don't know why he brought her here.

The sun sets and the night begins to creep in. A cold wind threatens the tent and towels strung on the guidelines. The sky and stars take over. The lights flickering across the water in Saudi seem very far away.

The three have pulled inwards. They quietly gather driftwood to start a fire, don sweaters and cook coffee. Daniel cuts a hole in the side of a plastic bottle, fills the bottom with sand and inserts a candle. The flame burns brightly.

They hold the steaming cups of coffee and stare into the hollows of sweet darkness as if the answers lay there. They don't look at each other and no one breaks the silence as the night grows blacker and the tapestry of stars draws their attention upwards. Daniel, surprising himself, feels tears in his eyes. Arlene goes to bed first, and not used to sleeping alone, tosses fitfully in the van. Mussa thinks perhaps he will not leave in the morning.

Chapter 2

Mussa sees himself as belonging to the universe. He is connected to past, present and future. From childhood he learned that he is part of a people and without that people he is with the elements - the wind, the sun and the stars. He does not understand the western concept of alone. He knows there is always interplay - energy and communication. Having read about isolation, studied anomie, Mussa understands the terms. But he believes we exist; we create around us; we are created upon. There is no separateness.

The village where Mussa grew up is nestled in the hills of Galilee, north of Haifa. It has a mixed Arab population, Christian and Muslim. The cobblestoned streets are narrow and lined with white two- and three-storey homes. Children grow in this pastoral atmosphere surrounded by aunts, uncles, cousins and gently rolling landscape.

Mussa's father always warned him not to get too close to Jews. "They are not to be trusted. You must centre your life on your village, distance yourself from the turmoil around you, tend the land. And when you are older, you will help me in the cement business."

But his father also wanted his children to get a general education. Mussa learned Hebrew in the public school, patriotic songs and some Zionist history of the state he lived in. The more his father warned him against contact with Jews, the more his curiosity grew. The Other became an obsession. On occasion when a Jewish customer was invited into their home, Mussa would peek around doorways, eager for an encounter with the forbidden. And if he was caught, his father would switch the conversation to Yiddish. So Mussa learned that language too.

When he was older and began to travel to the city of Haifa, Mussa first experienced what it was to be a minority. As a boy of nine, waiting for his uncle in front of a building supply store on downtown Yaffa Street, a rowdy group of Jewish children passed by.

"Dirty Arab," they jeered.

"I don't know why they said that," Mussa told his uncle. "Can I bring them home to see how clean Mama keeps the house?"

The uncle smiled and didn't answer. There was some talk in the family about not allowing Mussa into the city but it was decided he could continue.

Mussa was his mother's favourite. She was from a wealthy Cairo family and had been well educated. Her youngest son was her most intelligent child, and as soon as he could understand she read to him - in Arabic, French and English. With his talent for languages, it was easy for Mussa to learn Hebrew and Yiddish. His reading gave him a multi-faceted view of life. When he visited the Holocaust Memorial and Museum in Jerusalem with his high school class, his concept of the universality of pain and suffering was reinforced. He was lost to the Arab radical activist movements. As the nature of the Palestinian struggle became clearer to him, he felt paralysed, unable to hold a conviction long enough to act on it. His mother, sympathizing with her son's intellectual struggles, convinced her husband to let Mussa attend Haifa University.

Mussa studied hard and the work came easily. In class discussions he discovered he was not the only one in conflict. He became eloquent as a representative "Israeli" Arab. Mussa was a popular coffee partner for fellow students and teachers. Soon other Arab students were asking his advice in personal and academic matters. He was happy to help, fighting with them against daily humiliations.

Though he himself lived in the dormitory, Mussa actively opposed off-campus housing discrimination. The Jews of Haifa were not eager to rent to an Arab. And when there was a disturbance on the West Bank, he joined in the demonstrations of solidarity at the university. But Mussa remained primarily a theorist. And the radical groups were always trying to convert or condemn him.

"I can't work for the destruction of the Jewish state, even though I believe it to be an artificial entity built on my people's homeland," he would defend himself over a beer at the Balfour Cellar. "The Jews were also a homeless nation, one that suffered and needs to rest and cleanse itself. They are damaged, psychologically and physically, and it will take generations to heal the wounds. Right now they are not sane. And they are at their worst here in this country - sometimes monsters no less than the Nazis."

A member of the Jewish radical left laughed. "An Arab with American angst problems. Have you thought of therapy?"

"I know you're being cynical, Daphna. But I did think about it and rejected the option. I'm not a westerner and that pursuit-of-happiness business can't be transplanted to this soil. Those psychological ways to make things appear better by changing an attitude are simply methods to prevent revolution. They are a product of a capitalist mentality. You and I are determined by cultures very different from the American one. Yet our two cultures are also not the same. You can't deny your Jewish roots, no matter how dedicated a Communist you are."

"Racist."

"That's not fair, Daphna." Mussa had learned very early that those labels were meaningless. "And I'll tell you why. Your view has been shaped the same as mine has - by your sex, your experience, the experience of your parents and grandparents. Just think about the American teachers trying to get Arabs to look them in the eye. They think I'm shifty. I find them offensive. Cultural differences are very real and they cause problems. And these differences aren't surface ones where we can just learn the others' ways and everything will be okay. Deep down we aren't all the same. Which means you and I can't battle together. And our futures won't be shared.''

"Mussa, I feel sorry for you."

Daphna spoke Arabic better than most of the Jews who had taken it upon themselves to penetrate the barriers. Her Arab boyfriend, Khaled, was also a friend. Their house became a sanctuary for Mussa where he could eat home-cooked food and enjoy animated conversation.

On campus, Jewish women watched Mussa, giggled as he passed, blushed and lowered their eyes when he talked to them. In the beginning he was frightened. He stammered if approached, dismissing even the thought of making love to a Jewess - a soldier in the Israeli army.

Before leaving for university, Mussa was married to Olfat, a girl he had known from childhood. It was his father's way of tying him to the village. On his first visits home he told his wife about the women's reactions to him and made light of it. "This is the degenerate state of the city. You're lucky I'm a village boy and pure in my ways."

Olfat laughed and rolled her eyes. "Come to bed, husband, and I'll show you how sophisticated village people can be."

But Mussa found himself thinking of Gila in his "Introduction to Statistics" class as he made love with his wife.

Later in the semester he made love with Gila. He liked her because she had no particular stake in the Arab cause - the only Arab she was interested in was Mussa. She was smart, funny and very pretty, and Mussa was delighted to be with her, even though his political friends ridiculed him and called Gila his "Polish Lady." Their relationship would have continued if Gila hadn't become pregnant. The abortion was no problem. Permission was granted immediately when the hospital committee heard that the father was an Arab. But Gila could not forget the faces of the Jewish psychiatrist, obstetrician and social worker who had sat in judgement - the look of condemnation and revulsion they all shared.

Border Crossing 17

"I just can't deal with the world out there," she told Mussa. "I've got to be free to find someone who gives me security. A source of strength."

Mussa understood. They parted friends.

After Gila, there were a series of affairs. Women were irresistibly drawn to his long hard body, shy eyes and sensual, moustache-draped mouth. He left a string of broken hearts, building a reputation on campus as the Palestinian Don Juan.

During the first summer vacation Olfat gave birth to twin girls. The couple had lived in Mussa's house since their marriage and his father now proudly supervised the building of a three-room addition for his son's family. Mussa's mother was delighted with her first grandchildren.

Olfat was tired, and as time passed, didn't regain her energy. Her initial sexual curiosity was satisfied and the birth had been difficult. She was not anxious to be touched again. The babies were healthy and demanding and Mussa was not expected to be involved in their care.

In the village he spent time with his friends. He helped in the business and listened to harangues from his increasingly politicized brother. He couldn't wait to get back to school where a new freshman class awaited him.

In his second year, however, his grade average slipped and he was invited by concerned teachers to counselling sessions where he was told he wasn't reaching his potential. By third year and the prospect of a permanent return to the village, Mussa was barely receiving passing grades, though his relationship with the faculty was better than ever. As he neared the end of his last undergraduate year, there occurred an incident of racial violence that was too close for comfort and he began to get severe headaches. The school doctors could find no physical explanation. When an especially severe attack occurred on a visit home, his mother consulted the village *mukhtar*. It was decided that Mussa must immediately return to the village and be with his family.

"The city has corrupted you," Mussa's father repeated the words of the elder. "You're suffering as a result of your sins. You smoke and drink, and though you think we don't know this, you've been with many women. You're being punished, and it's time to come home and live a normal life. You will have no use for a degree anyway.''

Mussa felt his future slipping away. ''You'd love it if I came home, wouldn't you? Then you could have me back under your control where you can correct my every move, make all my decisions, treat me like the slaves you've made out of my brother and sisters and mother. And eventually you'd give me the small freedom to behave in the same tyrannical way to my wife and children.''

His father, who was generally a good-humoured man, had first been white with shock at the outburst. Then he regained his colour and smacked his son across the face. Mussa lurched backwards, found his feet, stood and walked out the door. Later he found his mother.

''I will never come back into this house again.''

She'd been crying and now burst into fresh tears.

''He loves you, Mussa. Try and understand him. He knows no other way. Kiss his hand and let him forgive you. You'll both feel better and I'll have a peaceful home. Right now he musn't even see me talking to you. Please, Mussa.''

''You'll come visit me in the city. I'll talk to you on the phone when he's not here. That man won't humiliate me again.''

He tried to hug her but she was so frightened she wilted in his arms. His head was pounding.

Olfat was philosophical about the fight. ''I'm under your father's protection, Mussa. And you're not here most of the time. It'll be hard for me being without you and not allowed to mention your name. The twins will feel it too. But he's not a bad man. You spoke in anger and all it needs now is some way for him to save his pride.''

''And what about my pride?''

''You're younger, Mussa. And he's your father.''

Mussa felt he was about to lash out at Olfat too. So, instead, he packed his overnight bag, kissed his daughters and returned to Haifa to finish his degree, despite the headaches.

His mother visited her son and pleaded on her knees for Mussa to heal the rift. His sisters said they needed him to be in contact with their father about their futures. The fundamentalist brother sent a letter warning about the terrible vengeance that awaited him if he kept up his rebellious ways. Olfat spoke to Mussa on the phone with increasing reserve. After exams, he decided to return.

It took his father only a few days to raise Mussa to his feet after the morning hand-kissing ritual. Then he embraced him. Mussa was teary-eyed, and later when his mother was called into the room to witness the reconciliation, both men let their tears flow with hers.

For six months Mussa managed to return to life in the village. He worked in the fields in the morning and helped his father, brother and uncle in the business in the afternoons. The evening was spent with childhood friends - getting stoned and talking of memories. Sometimes they would ask about Haifa and about the women there. His headaches went away and the family breathed a sigh of relief. Then came a call from one of his professors.

Mussa told Olfat first. "I've got a job offer in Tel Aviv. It's working in educational T.V. They're starting to put more Arab content in the kids' shows. It's very good work, Olfat, and it pays well. I'm going to take it. Do you want a divorce? Do you want to marry again?"

She laughed. "What for? I'm the luckiest woman in the village. I have a family. I live in comfort. And my husband is seldom here to bother me. Why would I want a divorce?"

Mussa laughed too.

He parted with courtesy from his father. "I can't live in the village, Father. Perhaps later in my life I'll be ready to settle down, but not now. I need the excitement and the experience of the city. I want to be part of the bigger world. I know you felt the same way when you were younger."

This time his father gave his blessing. His mother cried and was proud of her favourite son.

"You will wither and rot," said his brother.

His political science professor had recommended Mussa as a bright and articulate young Arab who was willing to listen to opinions other than his own. Mussa stayed with him for a few days until he found his own small place.

The job was stimulating. There was a willingness to hear and to learn about the experience of Arab children, and Mussa felt accepted by the staff at the television station and at home in the cosmopolitan atmosphere of Tel Aviv. He no longer kept in touch with his political friends in Haifa. None of them would have approved of his leaving the village.

Soon he was sharing a seaside apartment with a production assistant, Michal. His headaches were gone. He was seen as a success by the village, and in Tel Aviv he made friends - Arab and Jewish - each struggling for a creative solution to living in the strife-torn society. Mussa was happier than he'd ever been.

Chapter 3

In the city both Mussa and Arlene accepted Daniel's moodiness as inevitable and his protective distance was seen as a necessary procedure. To cope, they reminded themselves of the less exaggerated mood swings in their own personalities. However, in this inter-dependent isolation on Ras Burka, his friends are less tolerant. They need him more.

The sun in the Sinai rises slowly out of the water, grudging its rays to the three sleepers not yet in need of it, sending its heat to recall the dew dispatched during the night.

Inside the tent, Daniel wakes first. He smiles at the canvas roof above him, feeling sheltered and defined by the boundary of green fabric. The staccato rhythm of Mussa's breathing also protects and he luxuriates in these perfect security conditions. He feels an urge to move closer to his friend, to hold him and be held. He immediately banishes the thought.

Mussa opens one eye. "Why are you staring at me like that?"

"You woke me up with your snoring. I was trying to send you soothing messages to make you stop."

"I was dreaming about an old olive tree that grew in the garden of my house. When I was eleven the family decided to cut it down. They said the roots were destroying the foundations of the house. That tree had been my friend, given me shade and comfort. I became hysterical. They sent me to stay with my aunt and when I came home there was only a stump. I didn't cry or react. They said it was the tree's fate to be cut down, and I said it was the house's fate to be destroyed by the roots. So, Daniel, who was right?''

"They were. Because that's what happened."

Mussa rolls onto his back, grabs his jeans and removes a pack of cigarettes from the pocket.

The tent is warming up and the air is stale from the night. Now the smoke contributes to the congestion. Yet both men are reluctant to open the flap to the world outside.

"And what if I'd burned down the house before they had a chance to destroy the tree?" Mussa asks after reflection.

"Then you'd have been right. You'd have created an historical fact."

"Daniel, you're such a cynic. Don't you believe there's a truth beyond our own actions?"

"Haven't you heard? Moral truth is dead. I personally think you were right not to burn down your house. On the other hand, your family would have said Allah willed it or something."

"And that's what I said to myself about the death of the tree. But I dream about that tree. Sometimes its roots are destroying me."

"No wonder you snore."

"Go make some coffee. Then we'll go for a swim before she gets up."

"She's not your regular Tel Aviv matron, Mussa. Or an American hippie on holiday. You don't need to attack her or be condescending."

"She's an empty bubble like all American women," says Mussa, and stubs his cigarette in a tin can.

Daniel crawls out of his sleeping bag, pulls on his sweat pants and shirt and leaves the tent to light a fire for coffee. He wonders if Arlene lies in the van listening to their voices. He blames himself for poisoning the atmosphere - that it is his own inner darkness that causes tension. He envisions events out of control and spiralling downwards, and he sinks into a gloomy pit.

By the time Mussa joins him at the fire, Daniel is in his cold and distant place and has forgotten to prepare the coffee.

Mussa tends the pot and when it is ready hands a cup to Daniel. "You could at least say thank you." He knows he won't get an answer. They drink in silence. "Daniel, if it's what I said about Arlene, it's ridiculous. I'm sorry. Is that what you want?"

Daniel hears the words but doesn't answer. It's like being under anaesthetic and hearing voices in the operating room that belong to another world.

I should say something, he thinks. Tell Mussa he is not to blame. But he sits staring into the fire, clutched by an iron claw from inside, a claw that grabs all his attention and strength.

"Well, if you're going to sit here and sulk, I'm going for a swim. I'm telling you right now though, I'm getting tired of you defending her."

After a while some warmth returns to his body and Daniel stands and stretches. Then he knocks on the van door. "Arlene, wake up." He hears a grumble from inside and knocks again. "Come out and have some coffee."

This time she answers. "Hey, this is my vacation, friend. A few days in my life when I get up according to my own clock. Go away."

She tries to go back to her dream where she was waiting for a messenger to change the course of her life, give her a sense of belonging and purpose. Now Daniel has wakened her and the messenger will never come.

I'm sick of everybody's stupid demands, of being somebody's mother, wife, teacher, counsellor. And I'm sick of building the new Jewish state. I want to go back to the U.S. of A.

When Arlene decided to live in Israel, her life gained meaning at the thought of being an element in the national dream. But lately she has trouble with definitions made by politicians. And Daniel's pessimism has made her even less hopeful in her aspirations for the Jewish people.

"Are you still out there? Now that you've ruined my bio-rhythms, go get the coffee ready."

She pulls on her clothes and joins him.

"Where's Mussa?" she asks.

"Swimming." Daniel hands Arlene her coffee by the fire. "It's not working out, is it?"

"What's not working out?"

"This trip. The three of us."

Arlene shades her eyes and looks over the ocean. Its smooth vastness tickles the sand. The sun warms her arms as she stretches. The wind ruffles her hair. And a laugh begins to swell in her belly until she can no longer contain it. "I'm sorry, Daniel." She can't stop laughing. "We're all so fucked up. With paradise around us and refusing to enjoy it."

She doesn't understand, thinks Daniel, thrown back into the claw. Mussa is right. How could I have thought they might be friends? She knows nothing about the walls we live behind. She wasn't born here.

"You do forgive me, don't you?" She sits cross-legged in front of him and reaches out to touch his arm.

He shrugs her off. "It's fine. Don't worry about it."

She knows he's lying but is afraid that she may start laughing again. She finishes her coffee in silence, and only when she is in full control does she turn to him. "Daniel, I care a lot about you. I won't lie though. For a moment our situation amused me."

"And when I was lying full of tubes in the hospital and the sun was shining outside, did you laugh as hard?"

"Of course not. We were surrounded by wounded soldiers, Daniel. There was pain everywhere. These moods of yours come from a place I can't see. It's hard to tell when they're happening and adjust myself to them."

Arlene touches him again and he lets her bend closer. They lean into each other, foreheads meeting, eyes closed. The iron claw retreats. If he could, he would cry. They pull away.

Do I know any grown-ups, thinks Arlene, or are we all like this, needing constant reassurance? Our lives are spent trying to prove that we care, that we love, accepting whatever developmental stage we're going through.

"Do you feel better?" she asks.

"Sorry I was so nasty. It's not your fault. I know you want to help. Mussa too. It's ironic. Here I am both the organizer of this adventure and the biggest pain in the ass. I hope we'll be able to salvage something."

"Make me breakfast, Daniel."

He goes to the van. Arlene's crumpled sleeping-bag makes warm vibrations in this environment that Daniel keeps sterile and rigidly neat. He pours some of her home-made granola into two bowls and adds condensed milk. He sets the bowls, spoons and paper towels on a clipboard he finds under the front seat.

Arlene is stretched back, balanced on her hands, squinting into the morning sun.

"Breakfast, madam."

She takes her bowl and spoon with a nod, then turns from the sea to watch the play of light on the mountains behind her. The uniformly brown crag of yesterday now emerges a palette of subtle reds, purples and oranges. Their beach is closed to the south by a rock embankment and on the north end by the shining white peak they passed on the way in, gradually descending to the sea in a cascade of white sand.

"Look, Daniel. The hill is a face in profile."

"And that's why they call it Shining Head."

She remembers the tattered flag and shed behind the hill. "It seems strange claiming a place like this for any one country. And why rub it in by sticking a flag here of all places? Why not let it at least feel universal?"

"Good thing Mussa isn't here to give you an answer. I suggest we just accept the flag as part of the background."

"Why is it taking him so long?"

"I imagine he's basking in the sun on another part of the shoreline, taking some time for himself."

She finishes her granola, then stands and pulls off her jeans and T-shirt, revealing an orange and black bikini.

A wave of anxiety rushes through her, a sense of loss. She takes a towel from the line and spreads it on the sand pointing to the sun, smooths on sun cream from toe to hairline and lies back facing the direction of the rays. It's the silence, she thinks. No radio. I can't remember eating breakfast without the newscaster reporting which crisis I should focus on for the day. And she lies on her towel worrying about her family.

Daniel makes himself another cup of coffee and stares out at the myriad blues of the sea. Water is supposed to have a calming effect, he thinks. But what would it be like to drown, how much gasping and struggling does it take before one becomes unconscious?

"Daniel, is it okay if I take off my top? I don't want to do it when Mussa is around."

"Sure." He has been to the nude beach with Arlene, Yossi and the children and learned to hide his shyness.

"Just tell me if you see him coming."

Arlene pulls the black string and her breasts fall free. She swings her hair to the side and lies on her back, leaving Daniel free to study her. Her light brown breasts are tan all the way to the nipples, though not as much as the rest of her, and Daniel remembers that other shore filled with brown bodies - so many that nakedness became commonplace. Her nipples are warm pink and long and Daniel realizes he is aroused. He turns his eyes back to the sea not to abuse her trust.

The feeling of warm sun on her breasts returns Arlene to thoughts of her girls, Tali and Maya, and her son, Tamir. The little boy was conceived three years ago after the reconciliation with her husband. Yossi saw that his new relationship was only repeating patterns of the old one and elected to return to his family. The couple grew closer.

Yossi should have come on this trip, she thinks.

"The Sinai was ours since time immemorial," said Yossi, "and the politicians at Camp David betrayed us into giving it to the Egyptians. How can I visit now? It's as if a loved one were captured by the enemy and you're asking me to watch her being violated. It's not for me."

Yossi did not approve of Arlene's friendship with Daniel but he tolerated it. He thought Daniel was unstable - neither married nor a homeowner. And he was a bad influence on Arlene, making her restless and unhappy. But Yossi accepted Daniel as a surrogate brother-in-law, substitute family for his wife whose relatives were all in America. So Yossi sighed and wished Arlene a good trip, knowing that his mother would help with the children while Arlene was away. It was no secret that she ran the household more to his taste than did his working wife.

Thinking of her children, Arlene is aware of the hours she has forgotten they existed. What kind of mother is that? she accuses herself. And now they are in my head and there is such longing.

Mussa lies on a beach to the south. He has pulled himself onto the sand after an exhausting swim through fish-filled water and is dozing in the morning sun. He dreams he's riding on a black horse and a storm rages around him. He has to reach the next village. The lives of many families depend on him. The dream is so vivid he can feel his leg muscles gripping the sides of the horse, and the wind and rain whipping his face. He wakes while riding, not having reached his destination. It takes him a few minutes to realize where he is.

Ah yes, Daniel. I should be more patient with him. I know his black holes. But why is he triggered by such abstract things? People become depressed because their life's work is over or their family destroyed. Daniel disappears into despair over thoughts in his head.

On his way back Mussa picks up a discarded plastic bag and wading into the water, scoops small fish into it. He also gathers a few brilliantly coloured sea shells and some coral to bring back to Michal. He climbs the rocks protecting Ras Burka, and seeing two bodies stretched out in the sun, he slows his step. Arlene is half-naked. Mussa sucks in his breath, fantasizing himself crushed against her. He calls out, "Get dressed. You shouldn't lie around like that."

She jumps to a sitting position and crosses her arms over her breasts. "Daniel, why didn't you wake me when you saw him coming?"

"It's not me you should be worried about," says Mussa. "What about that flag up there? That's a lookout post with Egyptian soldiers guarding it. I believe we must respect the culture of the country we're visiting."

"Oh Jesus, Mussa. I didn't know."

She struggles to fasten the bikini string. "Why didn't you tell me soldiers were there? And you, Daniel?"

"Shit, don't go all crazy. I thought you knew," Daniel answers.

"You see them if you swim out in that direction. If they're not in the shed." Mussa now feels guilty at alarming her. He watches her fingers fumbling to close the clasp.

She's a child learning to tie her shoelaces. My daughters trying their first hair ribbons.

Arlene stretches out her hand to Daniel. "Come for a swim. You haven't even been in the water. You might as well have set up your camping equipment in your backyard in Tel Aviv."

They run into the ocean until the water is too deep to stand, then dive beneath the surface.

Chapter 4

Daniel is a survivor of his parents' past. And the past is his legacy. To cut loose and forget is to deny meaning to that experience, make tragedy into farce. But for him to hang on is to remember and to drown. Daniel believes in order to survive he must leave the past behind, as his parents did before him. They both made choices to leave those that were doomed and to move on. But the doomed lived on in the survivors and were reborn with their children - with Daniel. He knows he has no choice but to carry them. They will clutch at him forever.

At Auschwitz Daniel's father lost mother, father, brothers, sisters, a wife and three small children. He shovelled some of his own family's bodies into the oven. Daniel's mother, also left with no family, was saved by undergoing a number of "gynecological experiments" in the concentration camp. After the war, though told in Israel that there was little hope she would ever have a child, her determination and courage convinced her surgeon to perform a number of painful operations and treatments which finally resulted in the births of her two children - proof for her that Hitler had not won and her own survival was justified.

Daniel's father had been a silent partner in the procreation project, neither encouraging his wife nor denying her. His relationship to his children after they were born continued to be distant, never allowing him to again take on emotional responsibility; but he provided for his family's security, working long hours as manager of a large men's clothing store.

Once, before the war, he had been a gentle and caring man. But now at night in bed with his wife he seldom touched her, though he would often lie awake hours listening to her quiet crying. On occasion, after waking from a violent nightmare, gasping for breath, he would pour his painful need into her.

Sometimes he would beat the children. He would be eclipsed by a strange frenzy where his eyes seemed to turn in on themselves. This frightened them more than the actual blows. The attacks had no correlation to their behaviour, though the children believed they did. They also happened without warning, when they were quietly studying in their room or at the table in the middle of a meal.

As they grew older, they learned to dodge out of the way and lock themselves in the bathroom until he calmed down. But not until they left home could Daniel and his sister avoid the times when they were yanked by the hair from a warm bed and hurled onto the cold marble floor.

Daniel has fond memories of his mother, especially pre-kindergarten when the house emptied in the morning, father leaving for work and sister sent off to school. He and his mother would climb into her bed for an hour or so before she would have to get up again to do her housework. The house was still and relaxed in a way it could never be when his father was around. His sister's presence too added a mother-daughter tension that he could not penetrate.

Alone with him, Daniel's mother was his alone and she would tell him stories from her childhood before the war - about trips to the river for picnics, concerts and parties. There were funny stories about his grandparents and aunts and uncles he would never know. She especially talked about her younger brother, also named Daniel, whom she had last seen when he was sent to get sandwiches at the train station during the family's attempt at escape. She would hold him close and he would feel her tears slide down the back of his neck, and he would cry too.

"My precious baby," she would whisper in his ear. "My Daniel, who has saved me from the lion's den."

And he would whisper back, "I love you, Mama."

When the time came to start Daniel in school, his mother knew she must prepare him. "You're a big boy now and you must go and play with other children. Meet people of your own age, not just be around your family. I'm very proud of how big and brave you are."

At the beginning he tried to be like the others. When he cried he learned to do it so softly that no one ever knew. He practised in a mirror, keeping his face still when something upset him. And he learned to pay attention to lessons so that he could get by until it was time to go home. In the afternoon the tears came in torrents - so many that a neighbour handed him a green glass bottle in which to collect them. Daniel got the message.

He was a loner, giving a quick sarcastic retort to any gestures of friendship. When invited to a child's birthday party, he would stand on the side looking bored and disdainful while others played games. Mothers stopped inviting him. When he fell in the playground and cut his leg on broken glass, children laughed. He didn't react.

Daniel understood how others saw him. He knew he was different, that something was wrong with him. He was sure it was because others had homes filled with warmth and caring, and families who went to concerts and on picnics by the river.

He considered suicide while in high school and avidly read newspaper items on the subject, savouring details of procedure and technique. When the Holocaust was taught that year, Daniel was drawn to stories of those who had taken poison to end their lives before being removed to the ghetto or concentration camp. This would have been his choice - to die with a measure of dignity before the enemy could degrade him. He would not have fought for his life. He knew that the fight to remain alive, the one his parents had waged, had ultimately been doomed to failure. As Daniel saw it, he was the product of the union between a slave and an experimental animal, both of whom had died in the Holocaust.

Later on, Daniel discovered drugs. Through buying and some selling, he also found a group of people, students at the school, who thought that life was meant to be enjoyed. He gradually saw he could make conversation with people and even spark interest in the opposite sex.

"Why are you always watching? What do you see?" asked Anat, one of the younger girls.

"What's to see? A bunch of stoned freaks."

She looked hurt.

"No reason to cry about it. I didn't mean anything personal."

She got up to leave. He grabbed her hand and she lost her balance. They ended up necking on the pillows and Daniel discovered another pleasure. After that, it was assumed they were going together. He drew Anat more and more into his own detachment, ridiculing her if she turned to others.

"What do you see in Shimon? How can you laugh at his moronic jokes?"

Alone at Anat's parents' apartment, necking soon turned to intercourse. For that brief time Daniel felt alive. And afterwards there were those gentle seconds when his large body clung to Anat's small frame. In public, Daniel was cold to her, never showing affection. If she complained, he lectured.

"Why are you still caught up in all those rituals? I won't act in a prescribed way, talk in formulas and clichés."

"Daniel, if you don't want to see me anymore why don't you just say it."

"Maybe I don't."

She went away and he was relieved. There were other girls.

Daniel passed his matriculation exams and spent the three months until his army induction at the beach and a friend's apartment. He came home only to give his mother the dirty laundry. His father had stopped speaking to him in the spring after his refusal to spend Passover seder with the family. His sister moved to Jerusalem.

Daniel looked forward to the army. His crowd had plans to manage their four years together, maintaining a low profile, never volunteering for anything and doing their best to stay out of action. But Daniel was sifted out and put in a group entering officers' training school. He purposely failed his first set of exams and reached such levels of passivity in his behaviour that he served three days in jail for insubordination before being transferred to another unit. There he was reunited with his friends, who gained access to marijuana and hashish.

His young commanding officer treated him like another cog in the army machine and assigned him to physical labour. At night he would join the huddled clumps of men in the field, either freezing in the winter mountain snows or being eaten alive by summer insects. Everything was on automatic and his mind spun into oblivion.

On leave, Daniel would sleep in endless stretches at his parents' house and occasionally go out with somebody's sister, where long silences would be followed by crude grappling which sometimes ended in bed. After one unhappy encounter, the girl was furious with her brother for setting her up with this "machine," and word went around that Daniel was peculiar.

The brothers stopped arranging dates for him, and Daniel withdrew from his high school crowd at the base. He got stoned alone and was on the verge of doing serious time in the army jail when he was saved by the surprise attack of the Yom Kippur War and sent to the front instead.

Two men in the unit died, one of them very slowly. Daniel handled their deaths and cried at the funerals with the others. Camaraderie was re-established and the soldiers went back into action with a fierce determination that death wouldn't happen to them.

For a few weeks Daniel felt connected. Time was organized and there was an intense feeling of tenderness and caring in the unit. They were living life on its edge. When he came home on leave, strangers patted him on the back and wished him well. Daniel wasn't even embarrassed by his parents' proud smiles at their handsome son with his Uzi.

But the sombre mood of this war finally reached Daniel too. The Arab forces had come close to destroying the country. Israel was vulnerable and the era of the superhero was over.

After his four years of duty and release back to civilian life, Daniel followed the advice of a family friend and took a computer course in Tel Aviv. This led to a job with an accounting firm. He was still plagued with chronic sleeping problems and often woke up drenched in sweat. His mind drifted again to thoughts of suicide. During a stint of yearly reserve duty, Daniel consulted an army psychiatrist who listened to his complaints and prescribed large doses of valium. He tried the drug but preferred the effect of marijuana.

Daniel was recalled to active duty at the outbreak of the Lebanon War. He functioned well until one night on the Israeli news, after a movie about a Jewish boy and his grandfather in Montreal, he saw some film clips that drove him to despair. They were shots of the refugee camps of Sabra and Shatilla - bodies being pulled from the rubble by Red Cross workers, the form of a small child outlined by the blanket covering him. The story of possible Israeli government collusion in this massacre left him defenceless.

Shortly after, Daniel was sent as part of a back-up force for a group trained to comb village houses looking for hidden snipers. As he stood immobile guarding a family of nine with their hands behind their heads, he was shot in the back.

"You're alive. You're going to be fine. Daniel, you're fine." His mother's voice brought him back to consciousness after spinal surgery.

"Oh, shit," he said.

He spent his recovery period entertaining the nurses. Everyone was impressed at how cheerful he was, how few problems he gave the staff. His smoking friends smuggled in stuff, and even a couple of girlfriends came to wish him well. Mussa and Arlene were there often. And on his recovery, his parents bought him the van. Paid for by some of their German reparations money.

Chapter 5

Arlene still believes in what people say and promise, the way she did as a child. If you make a promise, you're meant to keep it. If you break it, you better have a good reason why. She was taught that promises are the essential ingredient for the development of trust, that they are sacred.

In the byzantine milieu of the Middle East, she has found that people who trust are thought to be naive and that most promises made here are meant to be broken. More than by war, she is frightened by this cynicism.

"Maybe our problem is we don't have anything left to believe in. We gave it all away thousands of years ago," she says as they sit under their plastic awning, eating lunch - black olives, pita bread and canned sardines - trying to keep the sand out of their food. "I'll never forget the day Sadat was assassinated. I felt so betrayed. Like I did when they killed the Kennedys and Martin Luther King. It's as if there's a conspiracy to do away with anyone we can sanely put our faith in, anyone with a vision that's a universal one. On the other hand, people like Khomeini and Arafat die of old age. The ones who only see through tunnels. Why doesn't someone kill them? And get rid of Begin and Reagan while they're at it. There are no good leaders anywhere."

"If Jesus came again, they'd kill him too," says Mussa, spitting out an olive pit. "That's what the teachers at school used to say."

Arlene is surprised. "I thought you were Muslim, Mussa. What were you doing talking about Jesus?"

He smiles at her confusion. So many years in the country and still such ignorance. "I am Muslim. But my village is mainly a Christian one, so I went to a Christian school. Along with our other studies, we said The Lord's Prayer every day, observed Christian holidays and learned all about Jesus. After all, God's son and I both grew up in the same neighbourhood."

She laughs. "My school was pretty much like that too."

Daniel grins. "So I see I'm the only one here who was raised as part of the religious majority. That must be why I'm so psychologically healthy, why I'm imbued with such inner strength and confidence. Isn't it true that you both feel comfort and security in my presence?"

They laugh with Daniel, but Mussa stops himself and turns to Arlene. "You need to know a few things about who I am. I don't want you to continue searching for similarities between us. We are not alike. For me, you're an enemy presence. Even more so than my friend, Daniel, who was at least born here. You have your own country - the United States - and if you're unhappy as a minority there, then you must work for all minorities and do it with more understanding. You don't belong in Palestine. The United States doesn't belong here."

"Give me a break, Mussa," says Daniel. "You promised me. And let me remind you that we're in Egypt now, which makes us all foreigners."

"Some of us are more foreign than others," Mussa answers and glares at Daniel.

"Did the Christian Arab children pick on the Muslim ones?" Arlene asks hesitantly, trying to break the tension.

Mussa holds Daniel's eyes for a moment, then relaxes and turns to Arlene. "Yes, sometimes. Children are children. They have trouble with things that are different."

"No more so than their parents," comments Daniel.

"Now it's you who are doing the provoking, Daniel." Mussa sits up straighter, eases his shoulders and prepares himself for a match. "If you two are moving in the direction of convincing me that my objections to American imperialism in the Middle East are based on childhood feelings of persecution, I'm afraid that the attempt's ridiculous. The cancer of the Jewish state inside the homeland of the Palestinian people is at its most malignant in the form of American Jewish immigration. This influx of dissatisfied, spiritually bankrupt capitalists is the most poisonous of the Zionist diseases..."

"For God's sake, Mussa." Daniel's voice is urgent. "She really doesn't know how to handle this stuff. Look at her."

Mussa hasn't paid attention to his listener. He had been girding up for an ideological battle and here was Arlene losing her colour. She'd read the diatribes in magazines and newspapers, but this is the first time she is confronted. She takes the attack personally, not recognizing the rhetoric or her role in it.

"Take me home, Daniel. Now. I miss my kids and my husband."

Mussa turns away. He hasn't meant to hurt her. She was a sparring partner - programmed to fight back, react with a political justification for her own immigration, something about Hitler or her family in Russia during a pogrom. Then he could answer he was sympathetic to her people's suffering but it didn't justify the rape of another people's land. And so on. But instead of a sporting opponent, he has to deal with a woman nursing her hurt.

Daniel looks at him sorrowfully. "Fix it with her, Mussa. And, Arlene, give him a chance."

Mussa gazes out over the water to the hazier mountains on the other side. It's not right for us to leave because of this misunderstanding, he thinks. "Will 'I'm sorry' be enough?" he asks. "I didn't mean to upset you."

She shakes her head, and Daniel gives her an approving nod.

Mussa smiles. "For the sake of our mutual friend, I'm willing to call a truce. There's no reason to ruin our vacation because of political differences that none of us will solve. No one here can bring peace to the Middle East. So let's forget it, okay? Buddies?''

He holds out his hand but she doesn't move.

''It's not enough, Mussa. I can't just put it away. If you hate me, how can we be here, isolated and dependent on each other?''

He looks shocked. ''I don't hate you.''

Daniel watches him.

''That was politics.'' His voice is soft. ''I barely know you, the person. But I am willing to try.''

She hesitates, wanting to believe him. ''That'll do for now, Mussa. But it's not over yet.''

''We all badly needed a vacation,'' says Daniel. ''And I wanted you two with me. But I'm afraid I didn't consider much beyond that. You told me, Arlene, that you and Mussa were both at the demonstration against the Lebanon War, so I thought the politics thing wouldn't be an issue.''

''We weren't together. We saw each other there, that's all.''

''Everybody was at that demonstration,'' says Mussa. ''But that doesn't mean we aren't on opposite sides of the barricades over everything else.''

The demonstration had been a shared experience for Arlene and Mussa. For days there had been a build-up of tension in Tel Aviv. Night after night, as the names of the dead soldiers and the times of the funerals were broadcast on television, Arlene sat hunched in her living room. Yossi had been called up to reserve duty and she lived in fear of the knock on the door announcing that her husband was dead. The children were pinched-looking and quarrelsome, jumping at sudden noises and running to the phone, hoping it was a call from their father. Arlene went to one funeral, the father of a girl in Tali's class. She took her daughter with her, figuring that an Israeli ten-year-old needed to cope with the experience. Tali wept, as did everyone, including the soldiers from the unit. Arlene held her daughter's hand as they lowered the body into the grave. There

Border Crossing

was only a slight intake of breath when they threw the first shovelful of dirt onto the white shroud.

When the grave was filled, they shook hands with the orphan and widow, then joined the others placing a small pebble of remembrance on the freshly dug earth. Arlene liked this custom and she liked sharing it for the first time with Tali.

While Arlene was feeling united with both mourners and protestors during the war, Mussa's isolation was at its worst. He had cousins across borders. He had Jewish friends serving in the Israeli army. By law, he could join neither group, and was left with the feeble protest of refusing to talk to Jews in uniform. But the main focus for his frustration and anger was the United States, for he believed the conflict to be an exercise for testing American armaments on a distant battleground. In this war Israel was merely a pawn in a bigger game. The organized protest inside the country was a smokescreen for the real power plays, and the cessation of this war would bring about no permanent change. Demonstrations were government-sanctioned procedures for diverting the citizens' attention. Still, after a visit to the village, he decided to catch one of the demonstration committee's chartered buses leaving from Mother's Park in Haifa. It would give him a chance to sense the people's mood.

From the moment Mussa boarded the bus he was recognized by old friends from the university, greeted and hugged. There was one other Arab travelling with them. A member of the Labour Party, he sat prominently near the driver, making a political point. Mussa had no patience with any of the political mileage the parties were accumulating out of the protest. No matter which of them was in power, things would be the same.

The bus wound down the coast through banana fields and orange groves. Mussa had sat down next to an ex-student he remembered from Political Theory class.

"It's good to see you here," said Yigal.

"Not many of my kind out for a thing like this. I'm not sure myself why I came."

"Because you're against the war. Like the rest of us."

"Not like the rest. You're the same as those kids in America who marched against Vietnam. 'Make love, not war' and other fine slogans. But my enemies are waging this war against my brothers. And my brothers are dying."

"So are mine," said Yigal.

"There's a difference, Yigal. You're the aggressor, we're the victims. That's not the same, is it?"

They sat in silence, each engrossed in his own thoughts. Around them were other quiet conversations that gradually died out as they neared the city. Traffic was backed up.

"Looks like there'll be quite a turn-out," said Mussa. "I think your demonstration is going to be very successful."

Given the opening, Yigal spoke out. "I'm also a victim of this war, Mussa. Potentially a dead one. Things are being done in my name that are abhorrent to me, and I've come to voice my objection. If my unit is sent to fight in Lebanon, I'll go to prison instead."

Mussa nodded his head in acknowledgement.

Outside, people were leaving their cars and proceeding on foot. They carried banners - in English for the foreign press and in Hebrew for their own. There were a few in Arabic.

The bus continued slowly to a central, reserved parking area and the excitement mounted. Those walking waved and greeted the buses whose banners displayed the names of their cities of origin. "Welcome, Haifa." "More power to you, Netanya." "Welcome, Holon."

Arlene was marching with a group called "Mothers Against the War." She had joined this protest organization because she hoped somewhere in Lebanon members were marching under the same name. Yossi, on a rare leave home, had urged her to become affiliated with an opposition faction within the more traditional Labour Party.

"The least you can do, if you insist on becoming involved, is have a group of people around you who have access to information. One day this war is going to be over and we'll be getting ready for the next one. Your well-meaning mothers don't understand this."

Arlene stood her ground. "I'm not getting involved with anything affiliated politically. My protest is a human one."

"You're still a naive American, Arlene."

The sun has made an indentation under their awning and Daniel and Mussa are getting ready to change the angle.

"Mussa and I may have been at the demonstration together," Arlene says, "but Mussa's right, we were there for different reasons."

"What other reasons were there?" Daniel asks. "In the hospital I saw interviews with people on T.V. Almost everyone wanted the war to be over. Very few believed anything could be gained from it."

"You're right. We were all against *this* war," answers Arlene. She is sure of her footing here. "But people like Mussa believe other wars have to be fought. They've got some cause. Or they claim it's self-defence. Or maybe they've got things analyzed that it's not a politically correct time for negotiations." She pauses and shrugs her shoulders. "And who am I kidding? You believe these things too. All of you who grew up here think like that. But I know that violence is always wrong. That's what I was protesting and that's the difference between us."

An American child of the sixties, thinks Mussa. But she isn't stupid and I know I can no longer ignore her mind and rely on teasing with our bodies. He lies back and smiles. "You have very little understanding of either me or the Palestinian situation. And in your place I wouldn't presume to analyze any of my reactions. You're not my spokesman. You don't know what I am for or against."

"Can we be on vacation, you two?" asks Daniel. "I didn't intend for this trip to be a political forum, though I should have been prepared for it. Arlene, don't be so sensitive. He's under doctor's orders to do his 'power-to-the-people' speech at least once a day or something goes wrong with his digestive tract. You're just supposed to applaud."

They laugh.

Daniel has his own memory of civilian reaction to that war. Before he was wounded, he saw his father follow the progress of the troops in Lebanon on a map spread on the kitchen table with little markers moving northwards as more territory fell.

"We'll get the bastards," his father had chanted. "Murder that Arafat and hang him with his guts streaming out over all those babies he's been kissing. Bomb the hell out of Beirut until nobody knows there was a city there. Catch every child murderer among them and make them eat their own shit. And their children's shit. And their women's shit. Hear their screams. Begging for mercy..."

He muttered for hours until exhausted and Daniel's mother put him to bed.

"I'll say one thing - you Jews put on a good demonstration," says Mussa. "Allen Ginsberg chanting to Allah was an especially clever touch."

The three put away the lunch things, moving with an efficiency of motion born of companionship and dependency. There are comfortable silences now. A routine is established - eating and sleeping, swimming and walking. The understanding is a primal one of survival.

Mussa and Daniel move the awning and stretch out in the shade. Arlene stays in the sun and reaches for *The Little Drummer Girl*.

Daniel feels the familiar claw closing his windpipe. He is aware this happens after he's felt tension. He takes small gasps of air, regulating the speed of inhale and exhale, until his heartbeat slows and his muscles relax.

Mussa watches the sea and remembers his first political demonstration after a boy drowned in a sewage ditch in the village. The rains had been strong that year, and though the children had been warned about the backed-up drainage system, they couldn't resist the puddles. It was only after three had died and the Hebrew newspapers covered the protest that the Israeli authorities put in pipes.

Why can't I live my life without filling it up with fictional characters, thinks Arlene. What I need is somebody's pen shaping my story, cutting out the insidious bits and advancing the plot.

Chapter 6

Arlene does not make friends easily. She cannot be casually involved. And because she lives a life plugged into others' realities, she must be careful whom she loves.

She was raised in Queens, New York, and the quiet order of its tree-lined streets and identical bungalows. The youngest of three children, she was allowed the most time for growing up and she used it to the maximum. In elementary school she was even put back a grade to allow her to "catch up." A moody child who loved to read, she would devour books at home but at school she wasn't able to answer analytical questions. The teachers often accused her of neglecting her school work. She learned to doubt her intelligence.

The neighbourhood was a mixed Jewish-Gentile one and the demarcations were rigid. Though neither religious group was observant, parents clung in friendships within their own community. Jewish and Gentile children only played with their own. When she began kindergarten, Arlene developed an aversion to the Jewish children. She didn't like their appearance, she didn't like their manners, and their way of talking embarrassed her. With her delicate bone structure, she could easily pass for Gentile. And she chose this option.

Shy and withdrawn, she hovered near the non-Jewish children, and they accepted her. Her parents were not known to their parents. Her father worked in Manhattan and was not active in the community, and her mother was a homebody who stayed within defined parameters. The Gentiles assumed she was one of them, and the Jews left her alone.

When she was ten years old, she asked her mother about Jesus.

"Is he really the son of God?"

"Of course not. It's a silly superstition, something people have made up, like Santa Claus and the Tooth Fairy."

"Then why do so many people believe in him?"

"Goyim like magic," her mother said.

"I like magic."

"I know," said her mother. "That's why you're doing so badly at school. Jews do well in school. Goyim like magic."

"They also said it was the Jews who killed Jesus."

"Who says?"

"My friends at school. They caught Marty Cohen and pulled his pants down and said he killed Jesus."

"You were there when they did this?"

"Not really."

There was a terrible expression on her mother's face, like somebody had hit her. She grabbed Arlene's arm and held on too hard. "Arlene, you better tell me exactly what happened."

She had never seen her mother so upset. It scared her and she started to cry.

"I didn't do anything, Mommy. I just stood there. He was crying and they finally left him alone."

"Shhh. It's okay, honey. It's not your fault."

Her mother told Arlene the story of Jesus, the Jewish rabbi who alienated himself from his people, claiming he was the son of God. And she also told her about Jewish persecution and Hitler and how it could never be so terrible again. And then she asked Arlene who her friends were.

Arlene told her.

Border Crossing

"Jews have finally learned we have to stick together and you must learn this too," said her mother. "Now we have our own country called Israel and we can hold our heads up with pride. No one will ever get away with hurting a Jewish child again."

Arlene was interested and asked questions. Her parents realized their negligence in not fostering the children's Jewish education, and her grandmother was horrified when her mother repeated Arlene's story.

Arlene was sent to Sunday School. There she fell in love with Avi, her teacher, and decided she was, after all, a Jew. However, when she again heard the taunting of a Jewish child on the playground, Arlene thought it wise not to mention the incident to her parents.

She would seldom see her father during the week. Often he would work on Saturdays too. On the weekend he slept late and then puttered around the house. He looked forward to a comfortable retirement where he would concentrate on his golf and enjoy his grandchildren.

Arlene's mother was always occupied with tasks. She was an obsessive cleaner and though she could afford help, preferred to do everything herself, cherishing the hours when the family was gone and she lovingly prepared her home for their return. She sewed and knitted and kept her children outfitted in the latest styles. If at times she felt unappreciated, she would talk on the phone with her sister and they would laugh together at their shared "misery."

"Don't tell Mama you're unhappy. She'll only tell you to count your blessings."

"Like she says, our problem is we don't have enough problems."

Arlene's older brother and sister, when at home, spent their time talking on the phone to their friends.

Everyone was busy and Arlene kept her ideas, conflicts and dreams inside her head. Until she reached high school.

Here she discovered she was intelligent, sexy, had writing talent and that it mattered to her the Negroes in America were being oppressed. She emerged from inside her books long enough to think about what she'd read and soar beyond the textbook material. Her English teacher encouraged her creative abilities and she was soon writing a column in the school paper.

Dating was never a formal practice. She slid into relationships through working first on the newspaper and later in the Civil Rights Movement, where she could express her indignation at the erosion of her idealistic views of her country. Increased contact with the opposite sex brought its own problems. She worried that boys were interested only in her physical being and not in her inner self. And sometimes she too was led by her body.

In her last year of high school Arlene made a major decision. She was not proceeding directly to college. Increasingly involved with a settlement house in the city, Arlene had been offered a full-time position there.

"She's planning to throw her whole future down the drain and go help the *shvarzes*," her mother told her aunt on the phone. "I don't know what's got into her. Arlene used to be so shy. I worried she'd never have a social life. Now all she thinks about is saving the world."

Her sister tried to console Arlene's mother. "She's young. She needs a period of self-discovery. That's what they're calling it now, and in our day girls didn't do it. Maybe she got the rebellious streak from Mama."

"I wasn't sure about that job on the school paper. I was afraid she'd get in with the wrong element."

Arlene's father was supportive. "You're eighteen years old and you can decide what's right. When I was your age I'd been out working nights for three years. It took another six before I had enough money saved to start my business. You have the advantage of not having to work. Just use the opportunities God gave you."

She moved into Manhattan to share an apartment with Marilyn, another woman working at the house, but moved out after a month to live with the project's director, Stephen. He had previously been involved with Marilyn, who remained a good friend and agreed to field calls from Arlene's family, creating an impression that the two women still lived together.

Stephen, the son of white, Protestant, working-class parents, was infatuated with Arlene and teased her by calling her his JAP. She was mortified and tried to explain that a JAP was an obnoxious Jewish stereotype that she detested. One night she confided in him that being Jewish had been a secret for part of her childhood. Stephen stopped teasing and took it upon himself to convince her to be proud of her origins.

"You can't work honestly with the people who come to the house if you're going to deny your own identity."

"I don't deny it, Stephen. I'm just not a walking advertisement. It's this concentration on differences that created the problems." It was her usual theme in her column at school. "We're all just people. With the same desires and needs. We have to stop labelling each other."

"Arlene, the very words you speak are so Jewish. Your universal view is a Jewish one. I see life the way I do because I grew up part of a white, Christian majority, knowing there were others who were different, but not conscious of it. You and some of the other minorities at our settlement house want to be accepted. You want to be like the rest of us. But we'd all be poorer in spirit if that happens. I want us to learn to acknowledge the differences in people, not erase them."

Stephen also decided to teach Arlene about her body. She was to regard it as a gift and not be ashamed of her attractiveness. If men reacted to her physically, she was to view this as a compliment. "No one has a right to treat you as an object, but it's wrong to deny an aesthetic experience."

"I'm supposed to feel okay about some staring pervert?"

"You know I'm not saying that."

"That's what I see on the way to work."

"We're not all like that, you know. It embarrasses me to hear that kind of talk."

They were constantly together. He listened and responded and made her feel alive and growing, both in their relationship and in their work. She began to assume they would marry.

Then, one night, Marilyn was murdered. She was on her way home from teaching an arts and crafts class at the house and was attacked by three black hoodlums, raped and killed. Everybody from their project came to the funeral, but the community gathering didn't help stem a rising tide of distrust. The next day Arlene came to work to find a slogan spray-painted on the wall: "Death to Jewish Pig Slumlords."

"I think my time here is over," she told Stephen. "I'm not wanted. It's your fault in a way. You made me come out as a Jew. Are you going with me?"

"Arlene, this is my work. This is a community I'm committed to. I can't just leave it when trouble starts. I thought you felt the same way."

"I don't want to die killed by the people I came to help."

"You're letting your fear take control. You're letting them win, those who want to destroy our belief in co-existence."

"I've been reading some Jewish writers and I think I'm beginning to understand where my community is. I also understand I'm leaving alone. Right?"

"If you leave, you're not the woman I want to be with. I was mistaken about you. You're not a fighter."

So Arlene went home to her parents' house. They assumed she'd had her taste of social involvement and would now get ready for university. But she surprised them.

"I *am* going to university, but in Israel. They have a summer program in Hebrew and I can start majoring in Jewish history in the fall."

Stephen's words had affected Arlene deeply and his accusation of cowardice hurt. She thought he would admire her decision to go to Israel and at the same time hoped he would be heartbroken after realizing how far he had pushed her away.

By the end of her first two years in Israel, she felt a sense of her own identity - integrated on all levels of her being. She even sent Stephen a letter. There is a purpose in every small act, she wrote, whether shopping at the corner grocer who has a tattooed number on his arm, or taking a school holiday that falls according to the Jewish calendar.

Later, when she married Yossi, a *Sabra*, and bore him his first child, Arlene felt as one with the Hebrew mothers in the Bible.

She finished her degree in Jewish history in between pregnancies and a growing sense of unease. The polarization of the country, with the growth of both the Jewish fundamentalist movements and the Arab protests at the inequality of their treatment by the Israeli government, began to gnaw at her spiritual complacency. She no longer felt part of a just fight and had heated discussions with her husband. He was unable to relate to her dissatisfaction. At times he sounded exactly like her mother and her aunt in their phone conversations.

"You have a beautiful home, a husband who loves you, three healthy children and even a job that has great meaning."

Arlene had joined the work force at an immigrant reception centre, counselling newcomers from all corners of the world about their adjustment problems.

"We travel. We have great friends. Don't you love me anymore?" Yossi asked when she continued to complain.

"I'm trying to explain to you that my soul isn't at rest and my life and commitment to this country no longer seem right. I've turned into a nice Jewish girl, Yossi, and the religious maniacs want to clear the land of Arabs and 'radical elements' to make it safe for 'people like me.' I feel sick."

"What's your problem, Arlene? You're not persecuted enough? That's the trouble with you Jews who've grown up outside of Israel in a ghetto mentality. You're accustomed to being the underdog, the downtrodden victim. You're not happy unless you're being oppressed. I thought your years here might have cured you of that."

Everyone in their social circle agreed with Yossi. It was only her friend, Daniel, who seemed to understand Arlene's discontent.

Chapter 7

Mussa and Daniel are often puzzled by women. Their main complaint concerns female ''pettiness'' - the interest in minor details of who said what to whom; tone shadings; what was worn; what was served. All the endless phone conversations discussing the effects and counter-effects of last week's arguments. And then there are those intense feminine clusters at parties that send them running for another drink. The explanation for Mussa's and Daniel's previous lack of understanding is that the fine nuances of human interaction occurred outside their field of perception. However, on the shores of Ras Burka, they are starting to pay attention.

Arlene half-wakes to find herself tucked between the men inside the shade of the awning. They are asleep, their bodies rising and falling rhythmically with their breathing. She wonders if they pulled her into the protected area or if she found her own way between them.

Mussa stirs and flings his arm over her to touch Daniel on the other side. She feels at peace, relaxed and close. With her back to Mussa, who is almost curled around her, she watches Daniel's face. His dark, disturbing eyes are closed and his usually furrowed forehead is smooth. He is in a nonmoustached period and his upper lip looks vulnerable and alone. The thick brown-blond hair lies tousled over his face and Arlene suppresses a motherly urge to brush it back. He wrinkles his nose and then rubs it with his hand as if sensing her intrusive thought. A slight breeze cools their bodies as the sun moves towards the mountains.

The shift changes at the guardpost above them, the soldiers exchanging a joke and cigarettes. They observe the buses, taxis, army trucks and private vehicles moving on the road to the Israeli border.

Arlene continues to watch Daniel's face. She would like to stretch but does not want to disturb the men. If I could somehow enter Daniel's head, she thinks, and find the buried mechanism that eases pain. And then the three of us - the trinity - would save mankind. She falls back to sleep, and the next time they awake simultaneously to find themselves cuddled and shivering in the gathering dark.

"Jesus Christ, what's going on here?" Arlene jumps up, laughing to ease the embarrassment. "If we've done anything unkosher, please don't tell me about it." She goes to the van to change into warmer clothing.

The men look sheepishly at each other.

"How did we end up like that?" Mussa asks. "I remember her out in the sun. Is this some strategy of yours, Daniel?"

"I have a vague memory, thinking she's going to get burned and calling to her. Other than that, my mind's a blank. I'm sure I behaved like a perfect gentleman, though. And you?"

"I slept like the dead. Had no idea she was even here. What the hell, I guess we needed the body heat. Let's get dressed and go for a walk."

The three stroll barefoot on the edge of the sea. Arlene reaches out to hug them both.

"I may never have been happier than I am at this moment."

Daniel and Mussa smile and hug back.

Their feet make sucking sounds in the wet mud and occasionally a car sends a soft swish from the road. But sound

Border Crossing

is secondary as the world fills with the changing colours. The water has given way to the mountains which command attention in vibrant hues and then in dark silhouette. The three climb the rocks at the end of Ras Burka and see another camp fire in the distance, then turn back to their own site.

"Tonight I'm in charge of dinner," announces Mussa. "I have a surprise. Fresh fish. It was caught by me and it will now be cleaned and cooked by me. And wine. I did pack a few essentials before I left my place. I wish I could be a creature of pure spontaneity, but there's a plus to having an administrative side. So you two find a grill and I'll pull my surprise from the sea where it's being chilled."

In the waning light, Arlene and Daniel comb the road to the highway and find a metal grid that looks like it was part of a bed frame. They present it proudly to Mussa, who approves. He balances the grid over the firewood and stones, and places the fish across it.

Daniel brings his marijuana stash and Arlene smokes too. The sharp smell of cooking fish envelops them. As he hands Arlene her plate, Mussa places a kiss on top of her head. She shivers.

"Cold?" Daniel asks and smiles.

The small fish are smoke-filled, delicate and delicious. The white wine is cold and tart.

"I'll cook the coffee," offers Daniel, after they have eaten. "But, Mussa, you must tell us a story while we have it."

The stars blanket them and the fire crackles. They drink coffee and pass the wine bottle. Mussa stares into the fire and begins. His voice is deep and melodic.

"My father, when he was young, remembers a visit to his cousins' house. It is still there, in a village in what is now Jordan. At that time, by the river, there lived an old man. The old one tilled his land by day and gazed at the stars by night. He talked to no one and no one talked to him. His neighbours had long ago grown used to his silent ways and left him alone with his thoughts.

"My father's cousins said the old man had always been there and that he had always been old and always, except for prayers, remained silent. No one in the village remembered a time before there had been an old man. And no one had ever heard him speak. The cousins believed that in his silence this old one had discovered some secret to ward off death. They were all a little frightened of him.

"My father was a quiet and thoughtful child - at least that's what he says, though it's difficult to believe it now - and there grew in him a certain fascination for this man of silence. He was not disturbed but rather excited by his cousins' tales of witchcraft and devilry, for he is a firm believer in the scientific method and the investigation of phenomena. He was soon spending a great deal of time in his observation post, a perch in a tree that overlooked the old one's property. He arranged his hours in shifts so he could have an overview of all the old man's activities.

"The old one's day was carefully organized. He would rise at six and warm his tea on a small burner. At this point I asked my father how, perched in the tree, he knew what the old man did inside his house. My father paused and then answered he just knew. I didn't think this was very scientific, but was afraid to tell him so.

"Anyway, my father continues, the old man would get up shortly before four and heat his tea. It was very cold in that season in the mornings and he would stamp his feet and blow on his hands to keep them warm. He never had to get dressed because he was already wearing all the clothes he owned. Twice a week he would go to the public bath and wash himself and his clothing. It's important that you understand that he was a proper-looking old man, not bad-smelling or dirty.

"After he had drunk his tea and eaten a chunk of bread and some cheese and olives, he would carefully wash his cup and plate, dry them and set them on the counter. He would then take out his prayer rug and perform his morning prayers. When he had finished, he rolled up the rug and placed it on a shelf above his bed, and after glancing to make sure all was in order, went out to his property. It was a good-sized piece of land and he spent the morning watering the soil, pruning trees, weeding, raking, tying vines and mending fences, only stopping for the *muezzin's* call to prayer at noon.

"In the hottest hours the old one would eat from a pot of lentils that seemed never to empty and then sleep in the shade of his baobab tree. When it had cooled he would wake for afternoon prayers and another cup of tea.

"The latter part of the day the old man spent inside his one-room mud hut with the two windows left open to catch the afternoon breeze. The floor of the hut was covered with grass mats and carpets, the only furniture being a mattress, a table, a chair and a cupboard. On one wall was a photo of the Holy Mosque in Jerusalem and on another a painting of the Holy Mosque in Mecca. Every afternoon he would clean his house - shaking carpets and floor mats, removing and scouring every item from his cupboard, washing everything that could be washed. As dusk fell he would spread his prayer rug in his spotless home and say his evening prayers.

"Supper was the same as breakfast - tea, bread, cheese and olives. He then would light his water pipe, face the open window and smoke. At this point father would miss an hour in his observations because he would have to be at his cousins' house for his own supper. After prayers he was sent off to sleep. But as soon as he felt the other children's regular breathing, father would sneak out of bed, jump through the window and escape into the night. He tells this part of the story quickly, hoping those listening won't get any ideas.

"When he returned to his observation post, my father found the old one lying outside against the baobab, gazing up through its branches. His eyes were wide open, the starlight reflected in them creating a strange aura around his face. He was immobile. A bird perched on the old man's arm, and small animals scurried across his legs. Not a muscle moved. It was as if he wasn't there. When he grew too tired to watch any longer, my father slid down from the tree and ran back to his cousins' house, scraping the dirt from his feet before climbing into bed. In the morning the old man would awaken inside his house as if he had spent the whole night there.

"The days before the family was to go home to Palestine were growing shorter. My father grew panicky that he would not solve the mystery of this old man before he had to leave.

He convinced himself that if he could spend the entire night watching, he would discover a secret. He finally confided in one cousin and begged for his help. The two boys devised a plan. They received permission to spend the night with family in a neighbouring village and rode on the donkey in that direction. My father slipped off the animal on the way and the cousin continued, promising to pick him up in the morning. My father then settled himself in for his night's watch.

"He found a crook in a branch, and after spending hours together both he and the branch grew accustomed to each other. Munching on dried fruit, he felt a rising sense of excitement.

"The old man put away his supper things and went out to the baobab tree. He spread his prayer rug and knelt, forehead touching the ground. My father whispered the litany with him. When they had finished, the old one rolled his rug beneath the tree and lay with his head resting on it. He stared upwards and my father stared at him.

"My father swears he was awake the entire night, but my brother and sisters believe he must have fallen asleep. I will tell you the story as my father told it to me and as I believe it happened.

"The night was quiet. My father knew something was about to occur and was not surprised when he heard a voice from high in the tree.

" 'Boy, why are you watching me?'

"At first my father was too confused to answer, but then his scientific nature took over.

" 'I am intrigued by your life of silence,' he told the old man. 'I think you have a secret to share with me.'

" 'You are a patient and intelligent boy. You will be rewarded. Come with me.'

"He took my father through the air to a palace. Inside, men and women in rich silks and brocades lay on pillows around a banquet table heaped with delicacies. Most of the food was unknown to my father - proving, as he says, that this was no dream.

"As he and the old man entered, clothed in magnificent fabrics, the courtiers rose and bowed. They were ushered to the head of the table. Musicians struck up a ceremonial tune, but as they sat down it changed to joyful chording. People chatted and laughed and the old one filled my father's plate and his with sumptuous morsels. When they had finished, the sultan - for my father thought surely that's what he must be - called for attention.

" 'Please welcome this boy. His respect for silence has earned him a glimpse into the world that inner peace can bring.'

"My father was entertained by dancers, jugglers and magicians. As he fell asleep in the crook of the sultan's arm, he felt a soft kiss on his forehead.

"In the morning he was wakened by his cousin throwing pebbles into the branches of the tree. The old man was at work in his field. My father felt as refreshed as if he'd slept on satin sheets and feather mattresses. He told his cousin that they had been mistaken and that the old man knew no secrets.

"My father did not go back to his observation post. But on the day they were to leave, he went right to the old man's door. The old one greeted my father in silence and then he kissed him softly on the forehead.''

Mussa's voice drifts into the darkness. The fire crackles, giving off an intense heat that keeps the storyteller and his listeners at a distance.

Arlene breaks the quiet.

"That was beautiful, Mussa."

No one moves. Daniel lies stretched on his side wrapped in a blanket, staring into the glow. Mussa clasps his arms around his knees, eyes closed. Arlene, sitting cross-legged, watches them both and tries to send her mind into theirs. She is thinking of her father, as are Mussa and Daniel.

He must have been a child once, Daniel muses about the man who is married to his mother. He too must have had fantasies and dreams like any other child. He lived in Budapest, a city of culture and enlightenment. He read books and saw movies and went to concerts and the theatre. He must have dreamed of a world where heroes performed great feats to save innocent victims of evil. Once he must have cried when he was hurt and let his mother comfort him. Maybe he was a curious child - like Mussa's father - wanting answers, not letting it rest until he knew. There is no one alive who knew him then. No one to tell me.

Mussa pictures the village and his father reciting his stories to the twins. And what will my children receive from me? Mussa wonders. What sense of our past am I giving them? I've left them behind in a world I once belonged to. They are now part of my roots and not as it should be - me as their history. It is their grandfather who will tell them the story of his visit to our cousins' house, and the story of how the donkey fell in love with the neighbour's horse. And they will laugh and feel part of a tradition. And I, their father, will have vanished from their history books.

Arlene's father never told her stories. He had no time. She remembers her older sister urging him to read a novel and he glanced at the cover and turned back to his newspaper. He never knew about the other worlds, she thinks.

The stars are huge above the Sinai. They fill the universe and their patterns imply there is no such thing as random circumstance. It's growing colder and the fire has gone out.

"Arlene, get your bag from the van," says Mussa. "We'll sleep beside each other under the sky tonight."

They spread the groundcloth on the sand and place the bags on it - Daniel in the middle, Mussa and Arlene on either side of him. They slip inside and shiver, waiting for the body heat.

Above them the guards again change shift.

"The woman is now sleeping next to the men," says one. "Disgusting pig of an Israeli."

"Shhh, Mahmud. They are visitors from another culture. Make yourself a cup of tea and calm down."

Chapter 8

Living in Tel Aviv, Mussa, Daniel and Arlene had lost sight of cosmic proportions. They could not see stars nor hear sounds through panes of glass and city noise and had no chance to measure themselves against the universe.

But now the three on the beach feel secure. Mussa and Arlene lie as protectors on either side of their friend who has trouble sleeping. Mussa would like to stretch his arm across Daniel and hold her hand.

Arlene remembers the shiver of excitement when Mussa kissed the top of her head. She defends herself by concentrating on the threesome as an intensive-care unit, a life-support system that musn't be disturbed.

Daniel tries to control his shivering. He is too close to the tender place his tears are stored.

Eventually they all sleep until the sun wakes them. Then they stretch and blink in the early-morning light. They unzip the sleeping bags in silence, shake them and spread them out to air. Arlene goes to the van, changes into her suit, then heads for the sea where the men are already bathing.

Over coffee she finally speaks. "Could one of you take me to a phone? I need to call my family. Make sure they're all okay."

Daniel drives her, leaving Mussa to clean up after breakfast. The road to the highway bumps them back to city thinking and they turn inwards. Arlene worries about her kids, and Daniel's back starts hurting him. On the main highway other cars increase their awareness of the world beyond their beach. By the time they pull into the gas station, they are separated by a chasm.

"I'll fill up the van, get the oil and water checked while you make your call."

The heat bounces off the concrete and Arlene leaves the door to the phone booth open. She tries to compose her thoughts in order to talk to her husband. It is still early and Yossi will be at home helping his mother get Tali and Maya ready for school and Tamir dressed for the daycare centre.

Arlene can smell their breakfast on the kitchen table - grapefruit juice, toast, yogurt, tomato and cucumber salad. Now Yossi stands at the counter, making chocolate sandwiches for the girls' ten o'clock break. They are slouched at the table, heads propped on their hands, sipping juice. Tamir is banging a spoon on the floor. Her own shadow hovers in the background, retrieving lost sneakers and notebooks.

Putting the tokens in the phone box, she dials and waits.

Yossi answers.

"It's me."

He turns to alert the children that she's on the line. "I'm glad you called."

There's a pause.

"Do you miss me?" she asks.

He laughs. "Tamir kicked up quite a fuss the first day you were gone. The girls, however, are enjoying the bathroom mirror all to themselves."

"How about you?"

"I'm lonely without you beside me at night," says Yossi.

Daniel is wiping the windows of the van. Sweat gleams on his forehead. He catches her eye and they wave.

She speaks to her children, then Yossi is back. "Is Daniel behaving himself?"

"He has his moods, the same as he does in the city. But everything is muted. It's hard to stay tense with all this gorgeous scenery. Sorry you're not here too."

"We'll go to Eilat instead, to a nice hotel, and you can read and suntan while I enjoy the air-conditioning. I've got to get going. Tamir's just spilled juice on Maya's arithmetic book. Good thing my mother's here to clean things up."

"Well, if there's any emergency, I'm north of Nuweiba, on a beach called Ras Burka."

"Come home soon."

"Thanks, Yossi, for holding down the fort."

As she hangs up, Daniel stands by the office, counting out Egyptian pounds. Arlene waits in the glass booth, the sounds from home lingering. You can't be in both places at once, she admonishes herself. She moves towards Daniel.

"I thought we were going to lose you," he says. "Let's have a cold drink from the cooler." He opens the lid of a white freezer placed under the overhang of the office and grabs a coke.

"You build up a world," she says, taking a Sprite from the machine, "and learn to live inside it. It's got its rules and its ways and you become a good citizen. You feel successful because in your world you are. And then you go live in another place or with other people and it's like your own world never existed. You've got to learn all over again." She pauses to drink. "Do you have any idea what I'm talking about?"

"Why wouldn't I know what you're talking about?"

Daniel is crouched beside her, balancing on his heels, Middle-East style. Their view is of a small concrete patch surrounded by desert.

"You've always lived in the same place," Arlene says. "You're single. Your life is based in one world, Daniel."

"That's how little you know, Arlene. After the army I wasn't the same person. And after I was wounded I became someone else again. And then there are my parents who live on another planet. You think that immigration and marriage are the only eye-openers?"

Arlene sips her drink. "Why doesn't Yossi see beyond his experience? Why doesn't it make any difference to me that Mussa is an Arab and to Yossi it makes all the difference in the world?"

Daniel laughs. "Categories! Married, single, Arab, Jew. Survived Auschwitz, never heard of Auschwitz. As long as he sees people as concepts, then he's caught, stuck in exclusions... Why did you marry someone like that?"

"He gave me a structure to live in."

They walk back to the van, the handles sizzling from the heat. As they increase speed, the wind cools the vehicle.

Why am I interfering in her life, thinks Daniel. She's a wife and mother, and I a suicidal loner. It was selfish of me to bring her here. She's a believer in humanity, and I'm barely able to hang on to the few shreds of my own personality.

Arlene studies Daniel's profile as he drives. He understands more than most, she thinks. And yet he is so alone. If he would stop the van now and look at me, I would open myself up and we would make love. Anything to let him know how close I feel, how important he is to me. Be careful.

Daniel looks over. "What?"

"Nothing. Just happy, I guess."

"Good. I was afraid of you making that call. One of the kids would have whooping cough or something and I'd have to pack you off to Tel Aviv."

She turns away and fumbles in her purse for her paperback. "Daniel, do you think *The Little Drummer Girl* is anti-Israel? They banned it for a while." She tries to steer the conversation to safer ground.

He ignores her attempt and lets her read.

Mussa waits for them at the campsite, glad of the solitude. He fantasizes making love to Arlene, masturbates and goes for a long swim. Afterwards, in the shade of the date palm, he tries to write in his journal. The activity is new to him, encouraged by his girlfriend, Michal, who believes he has something unique to say. He is learning to put his words on paper, in Arabic when in Tel Aviv and Hebrew in the village.

Today he composes questions in Arabic. Is there anything at all that is mine, anything I can give without feeling I stole it? Is there anything I can take and not feel it was stolen to give me? Even my thoughts and feelings don't seem my own. What is mine? My body? Is that the only thing left to me?

He sees the van swing off the main road and hurries to hide his notebook among his things. He emerges from the tent as they draw near.

Mussa watches Arlene close the van's curtains so she can change and thinks about divorcing his wife. What if I were to set up a household with Michal in Tel Aviv? We could have a sense of community. Lepers in a colony. We could have children that were not attached to either side. Perhaps if we left the country...

"I thought she might want to go home."

Daniel shakes Mussa out of his reverie.

"What?"

"Arlene. I was worried her husband would talk her into leaving."

Mussa doesn't answer. All fucked up in the politics again, Daniel thinks. He's out of the village and yet acts like he's still there. We both know the end of the world will probably happen tomorrow and the rhetoric doesn't make one bit of difference. All the politicals want is to step on each other's faces until the planet explodes. So why make problems here when there aren't any?

"Anybody coming for a swim?" Arlene calls as she heads for the water.

Daniel and Mussa stretch out under the awning.

"Tell me about your father," says Mussa.

"Where's that coming from?"

"I told you about mine."

Daniel considers the request. "There's not much to tell, Mussa. I don't have a father. If you mean someone who told me stories when I was a kid, that was my mother's department."

Mussa looks sceptical.

"Wait," says Daniel. "There was one story he told. When I didn't clean my plate, he would tell it over and over.

How he and some other guys in Auschwitz almost killed each other fighting over a potato. It was a funny story because in the struggle that potato got lost. He'd laugh. Then he'd say that's how hungry they were and I should be grateful. Then he'd smack me.''

They drift for a while. Then Daniel says, ''My mother was there too, you know. In Auschwitz. She's not so bad.''

''Mothers never are,'' answers Mussa.

Chapter 9

Only once did Mussa flirt with the idea of violence as a political solution. And that was under extreme emotional stress. He believes that violent revolutionaries, once they've gained power, don't know what to do with it. They lose their psychological base. Experts at reacting to the establishment, they don't know how to initiate. Mussa would never trust someone like his brother in control of a government. But since he made his own acquaintance with violence, he doesn't criticize others for choosing its path.

It was his last year at the university. He first heard reports of the missing Jewish child on break between the lecture on social conflict and the seminar meeting in methodology. The last time the boy had been seen was the day before as he was hitch-hiking to the university on his way to a tennis lesson. There were signs of struggle and tire marks on the shoulder of the road. Search parties were out and the worst was expected. Mussa approached a group of students listening to a radio report. One or two said, "Hi, Mussa." The others looked at their feet.

"Do you think I've got the kid hidden in my room or something? Why the cold front?" he asked.

A few smiled, embarrassed, but one in a knitted skullcap raised his eyes and glared. "Perhaps you do have him hidden, Arab. We're all thinking the same thing, but I'm the only one with the guts to say it."

Mussa fought for control. To swing first would mean immediate expulsion and he knew that's what the provocateur wanted. There would be plenty of witnesses to say the observant Jew had only been voicing his opinion and the Arab had unreasonably and violently reacted to him.

Mussa let his breath out slowly. "Well, you may be spokesman for everybody, but I think you should make sure you have the right to speak in their name." Mussa caught the eye of a short girl who was nodding her head tentatively in his direction. "Are you with this guy?"

She grew a little in height. "No. I don't suspect every Arab each time something happens to a Jew."

She turned towards the self-appointed leader. "You have no right to speak for me, David."

She had a sweet voice.

Mussa stood quiet and relaxed. Other students were nodding their heads and the "religious" Jew, David, knew he was fighting a losing battle. He turned his venom on his co-religionists.

"This whole university stinks. You've all gone soft and it will be the downfall of the Jewish state. What's happening here is more insidious than any war. Your spirits are being broken. You no longer know who you are and, worse, you no longer recognize your enemies. Like the German Jews before Hitler. Because of you it will happen again."

"Shut up, David." This was from a tall student in khaki army uniform who stood at the edge of the group. "While you're spouting polemics, there's a child missing somewhere in the vicinity of your lecture. They're organizing student search parties. Who's coming?" He turned deliberately to Mussa.

"Sure. I'll help look for the kid."

But when the mutilated body of the twelve-year-old was found, Mussa decided to stay in his room. A note, "Down with the Zionist Entity," was nailed to the child's chest, and feelings were running high.

Through his window Mussa could hear the bullhorns broadcasting the voices of people like David, encouraging the students to take revenge. Police had been called onto the campus, but they did nothing to stop the incitement. Still, Mussa was calm, waiting for events to blow over.

In the evening he heard a scuffle in the hall. Opening his door, he saw five young men dragging a thrashing burlap bag down the corridor. And they were beating it with a lead pipe.

"What the fuck do you think you're doing?"

He raced towards them, shouting at the top of his voice for help. Other doors opened, people spilled out and the five took off. The bag was untied. Inside was his friend, Nasri - bound, gagged, stinking in his own piss and eyes white in fright.

A student brought Nasri a cup of water.

"It's all right, man. They've gone. You're okay."

Nasri turned on him. "Don't 'all right, man' me. Animals. You're all filthy animals." He knocked the water from the outstretched hand. "Will you be a witness for a complaint, man? Get the fuck out of here."

The Jews and Arabs on the floor separated. Nasri was led into Mussa's room, where someone else brought him water. He sank onto a floor cushion and buried his head in his hands.

"They took me by surprise. I didn't have a chance. They had me tied and gagged before I could do a thing."

Mussa prepared coffee on his gas burner while Nasri showered and changed. The attempted murder left them in shock. Outside on the dark campus a curfew had been called and the silence made things more eerie. Inside, the smell of coffee and cigarette smoke felt familiar. There was a feeling of safety and protection. They dressed Nasri's wounds and drank in silence. No one thought of calling the police.

Sometime later there was a knock at the door. It was Jofar, an Arab graduate student from the floor below. "We all better get back to our rooms. They're coming to do a head count and you guys look like a terrorist cell in here. They caught the three who killed the boy, so things have calmed down some. They were from 'The Brotherhood.' Three young cousins going through some kind of self-imposed initiation test. Fools. As if this kind of thing will advance our cause. The Jewish child's parents are calling for vigilante committees. One can hardly blame them.''

"Nasri was attacked, Jofar. They were on their way out with him in a burlap bag when we stopped them,'' said Mussa. "They almost made it."

Nasri nodded. "We're going to have to choose, you know. We can't sit on the sidelines forever. And I know I'm never going to let myself feel that helpless again.''

"There's no coming to any resolution right now," said Jofar. "But let's not give them a reason to lock us up or put us under house detention. There are too many of us under their control already.''

After they left, Mussa listened to the midnight news. The dead child's name had been Itamar. They didn't give the names of the three who had murdered him, but Itamar's father expressed regret that they were in custody.

This same "Brotherhood" had come recruiting to the village when Mussa was a child. He was ten years old when he received the whispered invitation from the older boys to come to the meeting in the abandoned shack in Feisal's olive grove. He and his friends had gone and been filled with dreams of rescuing the "homeland." There were games and a secret pledge and promises not to tell even their own families of their participation. Of course, older brothers already knew, but it was forbidden to talk even to them. They sang songs and practised survival skills with their teenaged leaders, all in the atmosphere of danger and mystery.

Sometimes stories filtered down to the young Brotherhood recruits. Stories of how older groups played different games with real people as targets. There was talk of a Jewish couple who had been found love-making in the woods and how they had been bound together. It was not until the following day that they were found.

Most of the children drifted away from the increasing military discipline of those meetings, Mussa among them. On occasion he heard stories of a growing radicalism in The Brotherhood - of new leaders from outside. But he no longer had access to direct information. He had never thought the games would turn to killing.

But as he washed the coffee cups, overwhelmed by the image of Nasri's quivering body, Mussa allowed himself to wonder if perhaps The Brotherhood wasn't right. Sacrifices needed to be made. It was them or us. Violence met with violence. The Jews themselves, with all their rational talk and education and achievements, ended up in Hitler's ovens. What counts in this world is power, the power to strike against one's enemies, to protect what one loves.

He rinsed the cups, but the smell of Nasri's fear would not leave him. He sighed and stacked the dishes, then wiped off the low table where his friends had sat to drink. He removed his clothes and fell into bed, pulling the sheets close around him. As he drifted into sleep, a loud banging made him sit up with a start.

"Police! Open the door!"

He pulled on his shorts, rubbing sleep from his eyes.

"You're wanted for questioning."

He looked at his watch. "It's fucking two o'clock in the morning. What is this?"

"You'll come now. With the rest of your friends."

They escorted him downstairs to a police van where the other Arab students from his floor were waiting. Nasri was among them, covered in purple swellings.

"What's going on?"

"You won't believe it, Mussa, but those maniacs who tried to grab me filed a complaint against us. Said we threatened them and told them to get out of the dorm. When they didn't, we started a fight."

Mussa shook his head. There was nothing to say.

When they got to the police station, they called the Jewish lawyer who had helped them in the past. He promised to come quickly. The police put them all in a cell until he arrived. After hearing their story and seeing Nasri's wounds, the lawyer was furious. He soon had them released.

"And what will happen to those criminals who were responsible for this harassment?" he asked the police sergeant. "Are they going to be chased out of their beds in the middle of the night?"

"Is somebody filing a complaint?" asked the police officer.

"I'd like to speak to my clients alone."

He gathered the Arab students around him. "You must file a complaint. Otherwise, they won't do anything. Even if the police don't follow it up, at least there'll be something on record."

Mussa's patience snapped. "You've done your job. Now stop preaching to us and get out of here. We're not going to get justice in a Jewish police state. We'll take care of our own."

"I'm sorry you feel that way," said their lawyer.

"No need to be sorry. You should understand. Your own people fought a similar fight against the British here. And if you hadn't trusted the machinery in Germany, perhaps some of that tragedy could have been avoided."

Nasri sat beside Mussa as their cab wound its way up the Carmel Mountain to the university. The lights of Haifa twinkled below them into the Mediterranean Sea.

"You're right in what you said, Mussa," Nasri told him. "We must arm ourselves for the battle. We must not be victims. We have no choice - we're already swept along in the struggle. Now we can only choose what part we want to play, either passive victim or active defence against the oppressor."

Mussa was washed in waves of fatigue, tired of the preaching, of the semantics, of being told what should be done.

"Just shut up, Nasri. I don't want to hear any more. A child was brutally killed today by other crazy, victimized children. Everybody's making it into politics. Just shut up."

They completed their trip in silence. But as they went to their rooms in the dormitory, Mussa put his arm around Nasri's shoulder.

"Hey, I'm sorry I blew up. I'm wired and exhausted."

The next day Mussa began a passionate affair with the girl who had stood up for him at school. He had long discussions with Dalia and Khaled about what had happened. And he helped canvass for a defence fund for the three boys who had been arrested in the murder.

"But not for the same reasons you're canvassing," he told Nasri. "You want to use the trial as a political forum, a chance to be heard and quoted in the press. I'm doing it because I need to show that those boys are victims no less than the Jewish one."

"That is also a political reason, Mussa."

Mussa smiled.

"I can imagine myself doing what those boys did," continued Nasri. "We know that desperation breeds violence, and perhaps if more of our people were willing to put themselves on the line, our struggle might be over sooner. In your heart you share my convictions."

"No, Nasri, I don't. I'm a talker, that's all. I don't have the courage for action."

"You're too smart to be a lost cause, Mussa. I won't give up on you."

Mussa shrugged. And he saved two newspaper clippings from that time - one of a Jewish child with a sign on his body, and another of three defiant Arab children in handcuffs. They reminded him of his dilemma.

Chapter 10

Yossi, Arlene's husband, accuses women of being indecisive. Arlene agrees with him. She tells him the reason is that women decide, without understanding the consequences, to get married and then realize their lives are irrevocably changed. They're frightened of ever making a decision again. And then they become mothers and have committed an even greater inescapable act, no less final than suicide. Yossi tells Arlene she is being overly dramatic. All he was talking about was how long it takes her to choose wallpaper.

They met in Jerusalem through one of her Hebrew University classmates. The friend asked if Arlene would be interested in going out with her brother, who was stationed near them and had a weekend pass. Arlene hadn't been sure. She'd had a couple of experiences with soldiers who knew they would be disappearing back to their units in a few days - watching them spend the evening shaking their key chains in their pockets in nervous speculation.

But Yossi turned out to be different. He seemed older than the others, not so wrapped up in himself. He paid attention to Arlene from the moment he saw her, registering her physically and then asking intelligent questions. He answered her queries thoughtfully.

It was early evening when they walked through Jerusalem's Jaffa Gate, the light breaking into spectrum colours after the solid white of the day. The man who sold them bagels from his cart sprinkled on zatar spice and they munched them as they passed through the thick stone entrance.

"I grew up looking over the barbed wire into Jordan and dreamed of visiting this place," said Yossi.

"It's hard to imagine what it was like before 1967," answered Arlene. "Borders usually seem reassuring to me, but a divided city is an abomination."

He laughed. "After 1948 and the War of Independence the building on the other side of the gate was half in Jordan and half in Israel. Now, since the Six-Day War, it's all in one country - ours."

They moved from the wide cobblestoned street to the sidewalk. The stores beckoned them with their crucifixes and Bibles and olive-wood donkeys.

"If you want to do some shopping, it's fine with me."

Arlene smiled. "I shopped myself out the first few weeks I was here. I bought birthday presents for everyone back home for the next ten years. And my father will have a new *keffiyeh* for every Father's Day until the turn of the century."

Yossi gently steered her down the stairs into the *shouk*.

"Well, we'll walk through the stalls to the spices, then find a cup of coffee in the Jewish Quarter."

The merchants called to them in Hebrew, English, German and French, but they kept moving downwards and past the hanging clothing and trays full of beads, bells, bracelets and T-shirts.

"I'm glad I'm not in uniform," said Yossi. "Now I can pass for a tourist and not a moving target."

"Don't you think you Israelis are paranoid? All the people want is peace and to get on with business."

"And that's why we love you Americans so. You believe in human goodness and the value of a buck. What do you say in the U.S. now? 'Have a happy day,' right? I wish your world view were true, Arlene, but it isn't. You've grown up in a country where war hasn't affected you directly. You don't know what it's like."

"You're forgetting Vietnam."

"It's not the same for those at home in America. For us, at home means planes passing over your head, bombs exploding. Even the American soldiers in Vietnam know if they don't get killed, they can go home. They're not fighting to defend their own land, in fear of extinction."

They had entered the food section of the *shouk*. The raw meat hung from hooks in front of the stalls and made Arlene gag. Flies crawled up and down the carcasses. She tried to hide her discomfort, believing that Israelis paid no mind to these things, but she accelerated her steps and they were soon past the meat and by the vegetable stands, on their way to the spices.

The light was fading rapidly in the narrow passages and strings of light bulbs were turned on for the late shoppers. There were startling sounds of clanking metal as some merchants pulled down the steel shutters over their stalls for the night.

Yossi took Arlene's hand and led her towards the bags of spices. The large burlap sacks stood open-mouthed on the floor, overflowing with coloured granules and powder. The smells of cinnamon, cardamon, anise, red pepper and turmeric mingled together. Yossi stood between two shops, closed his eyes and breathed deeply. He opened his eyes to find Arlene smiling at him.

"You don't hate me after my lecture?" he asked.

"It's true, you know. I don't know what it's like to crouch in a shelter waiting for the 'all clear' - stories that your sister has told me about your childhood. To be afraid of dying. But I'm improving. At home when I'd see a guy in uniform and a short haircut, I'd feel threatened. Here, I'm embarrassed to tell you, I feel protected, even turned on. And proud too."

"Now I'm sorry I didn't wear my uniform."

She laughed and they walked on, feeling closer. Reaching the bottom of the *shouk*, they turned and the atmosphere abruptly changed. The stone walls were cleaner, the cobblestones repaired, the shops filled with expensive tourist items. Everywhere were signs of renovation and building. They had entered the Jewish Quarter.

"We'll pay our respects to the Wall and then find our coffee."

The Wailing Wall, all that was left of the Old Temple built by King Solomon, was a mystical experience to Arlene no matter how hard she tried to fight the tourist board's calculated presentation. She knew she was being manipulated by the newly built, grandiose plaza, in the same way she was conditioned to feel pride in the Jewish army. In both instances, her emotional responses contradicted her intellectual beliefs. Arlene believed in God and Good and Truth and Justice, but ridiculed the misty-eyed sentimentality displayed on Veteran's Day in America. She hated war movies. Since moving to Israel she had also become angrily opposed to the male-defined religious laws that tried to rigidify life from birth until death.

However, as she became identified with the Jewish people as her people, and learned their 5,000-year-old story, Arlene grew afraid of losing her old convictions. As they passed the Orthodox men in their long black coats, white stockings and fur-trimmed hats, it was a relief to experience the same amount of repugnance she had felt for the G.I.'s in the States.

"Let's just look from here," said Yossi. "I don't like the idea of letting go of you while you hide on the women's side and I display myself on the men's."

"My sentiments exactly." She appreciated his directness.

They stood behind the barrier that separated the prayer space in front of the Wall from the rest of the plaza. An old man in Hassidic outfit walked by, twisting his side curls. Seeing Arlene's bare shoulders, he muttered, "Shame, shame." Yossi put a protective arm around her and she let herself be drawn to him. They stood facing the spot-lit white stones that rose above them and felt their own part in the progression of events that brought the two of them to the Wall of the Temple, a place that had been barred to their people by so many centuries.

"The men who fought their way here burst out crying when they touched it," Yossi whispered into her hair. "Nobody thought it still meant anything."

"I know. At home I barely knew I was Jewish. Yet here I get the shivers."

"And my parents are proud they've escaped the ghetto mentality. Instead of fasting like we're supposed to, we grill meat in the backyard on Yom Kippur," said Yossi. "I was raised to believe that the superstitions killed us off in Europe. Did you know that when delegations from here went to Poland to urge people to emigrate, they were ridiculed and thrown out? The rabbis called them heathens and communists. God was supposed to take care of everybody."

He guided her to a café terrace overlooking the lights of the Old City.

"They have a very nice blintz here with homemade jam and sour cream."

"When do you go back to your unit?" she asked.

"Day after tomorrow."

"Did you fight in the 1967 War?"

"I was in the north, in the Golan. We lost quite a few people up there. I got out without a scratch. I spent the next few months trying to convince my parents I wasn't dead."

The cheese rolls were light and fluffy and the jam thick with strawberries. They shared the plate of food, Arlene making sure Yossi had more than she did.

"I wonder what it will be like when I go home," said Arlene, sipping the strong coffee. "It will be hard to communicate to other people what I feel being in Israel. It's a strange paradox. I've never felt so Jewish, belonging to this ancient people that refuses to die despite all the world's efforts. On the other hand, I'm more of an American than I've ever been. That's how I'm seen by Israelis. And when I see myself surrounded by people from other countries, I realize they're right. Friendly, naive American Arlene."

"Why do you have to go back?"

"Why is everyone trying to convince me to stay?"

She looked into his deep brown eyes and saw he was hurt. "Don't take it so personally, Yossi. I don't like the pressure I'm put under about 'my duty' to stay in Israel. Especially not from people who are surrounded by family and friends."

"But we must say it. We need you. And most of all, you Americans. We need people with education and experience in democracy, who have not been scarred by persecutions. We need your optimism."

"You sound like the representative from the Jewish Agency who came to talk to us at the *ulpan* when I was learning Hebrew. And you know something? I agree with every word you're saying. But part of my being American is my concern for the individual. Your words are very meaningful in a theoretical way. But what about me, Yossi? Where do I fit in here?"

He paused, then made sure their eyes met. "Well, you could marry me."

She choked on her coffee, then regained her composure. "Are you after my purchasing rights as a new immigrant?"

"You're becoming a hard-boiled Israeli, Arlene. You better be careful or you'll turn into a paranoid native. As my sister might have told you, my family is well off and I don't need help to buy a washing machine or a television. And I don't work for the Jewish Agency either. So drink up and let's go."

He drove her to the lookout point across from the Intercontinental Hotel in Arab East Jerusalem. He didn't stand near her and she felt the loss. The city with all its historical demands glimmered below and, as always, seemed to pull her energy. She felt queasy and her body swayed. He came to her side and drew her to him. She hid her head in his shoulder, but Yossi reached down and pulled her face up to his. They kissed once and then again, bodies pressing.

"Come, we'll go back to the car and I'll take us somewhere more private."

His voice was husky sweet and she let herself be led. They drove in silence, enjoying the tension, treasuring the in-between time and not knowing anything but the movement of the car and the light from the dashboard and the promise waiting to be fulfilled. Yossi drove back to the Jewish side of the city, skirting the downtown, and out to a forested area just beyond the lights. He parked, then spread his jacket on the ground for her. They lay down and enfolded each other in their arms.

"Ooof," he said afterwards, his head resting between her breasts.

"What does that mean?" Her fingers stroked his hair.

"It's an expression of the end of one's capabilities, spoken either in frustration or ecstasy." He caressed her thigh.

"Ooof," she said.

They felt cold and put on their clothes.

"What now?" he asked.

"What I'd really like is a hot shower," said Arlene. "But I don't want to say goodbye yet."

"I have a solution."

He left her in the car in front of his friend's house while he went in to check. "It's fine. We'll go shower."

She didn't see the friend, who politely shut himself in the kitchen.

Clean and clothed, Arlene turned to Yossi. "I feel like we've lived through so much. I can't believe we've known each other just a few hours."

"I was thinking the same thing. After making love for the first time with a woman, I usually can't wait to get back to my place. Here we are showered and thinking about what to do next. It's like a married couple."

It was the second time that evening he'd raised the subject. The way he looked at her now, Arlene believed he meant it. Yossi seemed so sure, she believed he must have access to private information concerning her soul. Her old rhythms - telling her to take her time, not think in terms of permanence, to explore - seemed shallow and "American." He was solid and responsible, rooted to a distant past and a meaningful future.

"I'm hungry," she said.

He took her to a small, dark place permeated with the smell of grilled meat. When they were seated at the rickety table, he took her hand.

"I'm not going to let you go, you know."

"I'm an American, Yossi. If you start denying me basic rights - freedom of choice and stuff like that - I can get nasty." She softened it with a smile, but he understood.

"Arlene, you know I'm not saying anything that you don't feel yourself. We've shared too much tonight to play games with each other. I know you Americans. I know why you came to Israel and I know what you feel being here. You're not the kind that will go back to the United States where your life has little meaning. And I also know in your heart you'll always be an American. I love that in you. I have no wish to meddle with any of the things that make you who you are."

"But, Yossi, up until tonight I had every intention of going home after getting my degree."

"Up until tonight. Your words. Until now, you didn't know what your personal reason was for being here."

She blushed.

The meat arrived on a platter. Around the black, smoking chunks, the surly waiter placed smaller plates of pickled vegetables, salads, humus, tehina and olives.

Yossi filled their plates and ordered beer.

"*B'tayevon*. I know there is no word for that in English. Enjoy your meal, I guess."

This is what I've been waiting for, thought Arlene. For this feeling of "rightness" with a man and to know he feels it too. But I didn't expect this to happen here. I didn't intend to stay in this country.

After he had cleaned his plate, Yossi leaned back and patted his stomach. "Now for a cup of good, strong Turkish coffee and I will be a man at peace. This has been a magical night."

They waited for coffee and the silence became uncomfortable.

"I just had a disturbing thought, Arlene. I wondered if I'm fooling myself, that what went on between us tonight was only inside my head. Something I made up. I thought for a minute that you were playing with me, like the young girls do in high school. Perhaps this happens often in your life and tomorrow you'll forget my name."

She looked at him in disbelief.

"So why don't you speak?"

"Because I'm frightened by your plans. My whole life is locking into place in front of me and I have nowhere to move."

He laughed. "That's what's so wonderful! Can't you see? We're fulfilling our destinies. How many people get a chance like that?" He touched her cheek. "It's a joyous occasion, Arlene. A time to celebrate. Pick up that cup of coffee and drink a toast!"

She laughed. "I think I can love you, Yossi."

Chapter 11

Since early childhood Daniel learned to face the world by keeping his pain within aesthetic boundaries. He realized when a need was too glaring, people either pitied or shunned him. On the other hand, if it wasn't shown at all, they felt frustrated and useless. So he learned to measure his suffering into appropriate doses. After the army, when he re-entered civilian life, Daniel continued formatting an acceptable image for the future.

His job at the accounting firm gave him a good chance to start. Working in the office, he could study others and find ways to react in the adult world. He was determined to become an expert in everyday communication. He understood why people had shied away in the past and he wanted to change things. He was also still worried about his sleeping patterns - frequent waking in a trembling sweat - but no matter how he tried, they continued. At least he knew how to access his daytime personality and get it under control.

The office was in a dilapidated building in the centre of town. He climbed three flights of garbage-strewn stairs to reach the suite, but once inside he was welcomed by pleasant, modern surroundings - carpeted floors, fresh paint, good pictures on the walls, bright track-lighting, well-designed chairs and tables. There was a staff of ten - the boss, an office manager, a secretary/receptionist and six accountants. Daniel was the computer man, replacing the IBM representative. It was an ideal position, where he had his own area of expertise with room to grow in responsibility as the company expanded. He had a cubicle with a window in a corner of the main office.

"I'm the workers' committee," said a prematurely balding man on Daniel's first day of work. "We're a small office so I'm the entire committee. My job is to welcome new workers and to let you know the conditions. We were told you were interviewed, offered the job and you accepted. Salary, you've been told. There are other fringe benefits you should know about. But first things first. What kind of food do you like? We'll go out for lunch and I'll fill you in on office politics. By the way, my name is Ido."

They ate lunch in Tel Aviv's Dizengoff Centre, sitting at a sidewalk table where they had a good view of shoppers, tourists and lunchtime workers.

Ido was an ideal choice for Daniel's first foray into friendship because he always kept up both sides of the conversation. "I think," said Ido, "this is one of the main reasons I enjoy working at our place - being within walking distance of the centre. The secretaries get prettier all the time, and I can watch them to my heart's content. The last place I worked was a grubby little hole in the industrial section."

Daniel watched a girl strumming her guitar on the overpass in the middle of the open plaza. She was standing on a bench staring into the cloudless, early-autumn sky and whispering words to her music.

Ido followed Daniel's gaze.

"That's not my kind," he said. "I prefer them well-dressed. You know, career types with their own apartments and cars and that tough exterior. They can have a good time, ball you and be friendly afterwards without a lot of expectations." He paused to signal the waitress. "Now that kind up there, that's trouble. They want to move in with you the next day and redecorate your apartment. Once I had one who wanted to bring her two-year-old. Forget it. Might as well be married."

Daniel listened, enjoying Ido's self-absorption.

"I've seen your C.V.," Ido continued, "so I know you're not married, just out of the army. Barkai is not a bad guy to work for, as long as you get your job done. The big guy we hardly ever see. Does a lot of travelling abroad with his wife, and when he comes in, he holes up in his office. Once a year, around Passover, he has all of us over to his house in Saveyon and we get a taste of how the rich folk live - swim in his pool, eat his food and play with whatever new toys he's brought back from America. Last time it was a computerized racing-car set he'd bought for his grandson."

Ido paused to ogle some passing French-speaking girls.

"The wife's grandparents founded Tel Aviv or something. He owns property. Most of the accounting we do is for him."

The waitress brought them hamburgers in pita, chips, pickles and salad. They ordered two mugs of Maccabi beer.

Ido bit into his hamburger, spraying barbecue sauce onto his upper lip. He licked it off and leaned towards Daniel.

"Hey, look at that one. Three tables over. Now that's what I call my type."

She was laughing excitedly as she leaned over to say something to her girlfriend. Her blouse was cut low and the two men were at an angle where they could see one breast covered with a thin brassiere to just above the nipple. She was pretty in a made-up way with short brown hair that had been highlighted with blond streaks. Her legs were below the table but one assumed they were good.

"Would you like her?" asked Ido. "I'm feeling generous today. Go on. I'll wait here and order us a couple more beers."

Daniel smiled. He would rather have begun with the guitar player. "No, thanks, Ido. You go ahead if you feel like it."

"You have someone steady?"

"No, that's not it. I'm just a slow mover. Not good at starting table conversation. I take my time - watch, listen. Check things out."

"At that rate you musn't score too often. Besides, with a body like that one has, who needs to listen?"

Ido held up his hand to signal the waitress for more beer. The secretary with the nice breasts rose to leave and her legs were as good as they had expected. They watched her walk up the ramp to the overpass and disappear above them.

The waitress brought their beer.

"Shira, desk behind me," said Ido, "is already interested in you. She asked me if you're married. She's all right to tide you over for a while. We had a thing for a few weeks. She's a pro at separating bed and work."

Following Ido's suggestion, he dated Shira. Ido introduced him to others, and the two men shared information and phone numbers. Daniel went to parties and after a few drinks sometimes had fun.

Eventually, he had Mussa for more serious talk and later Arlene too. And when he was depressed, he stayed in his apartment, smoked and listened to music.

Often the phone was ringing as he turned the key to his door. It was always his mother.

"So how was your day?"

"Fine, Mom."

"Come on over and have supper with us. I'd like to hear about it. So would your father."

"I have a lot to do, Mom. There are all kinds of deadlines. I'm afraid I can't."

"Of course you can. You have to eat, don't you? We won't keep you long."

He could sense his mother straining not to pressure him, but he still felt like he was being choked. He held the receiver at a distance from his ear.

"Daniel, are you there?"

"Someone's at the door. I'll call you back."

He'd slam down the phone, lie on his sofa-bed and reach over to the small drawer in the side table where he kept his stuff. Head propped on a pillow, he'd roll himself a joint. He imagined his parents dead and wondered if he would then be normal. Maybe he could leave the country, go to the United

States. All their suffering and the son ends up a taxi-driver, like the rest of the Israelis in New York.

Sometimes he'd dial the number and tell his mother he was coming after he showered and shaved and took a short nap.

It was hard to breathe in his parents' apartment. His father kept the windows shut so the neighbours wouldn't overhear any conversations. There was never enough air. As he entered, he could smell the aroma coming from the kitchen. His mother loved to cook and always had a freezer full of delicacies that she would take out and heat for guests. Her husband was not interested in "fancy food" and she didn't enjoy cooking for herself. Alone, the couple devoured huge quantities of bread. His mother also had a sweet tooth.

Daniel's visits, with minor variations, were always the same.

"Hi, Dad," Daniel calls to the stout, balding man peering over the newspaper. "Be with you in a minute." He goes to his mother in the kitchen and kisses her on the cheek.

"I'm so glad you could come, Daniel. We never see you anymore. People ask how you're doing, how you are, and I hardly know what to tell them. Your sister says she doesn't hear from you either."

"So what's new?" He smiles and licks the spoon she holds out to him. "Delicious."

"Go in and talk to your father. He hasn't been well. His stomach is troubling him again."

"Has he been to the doctor?"

"You know the only way to get him to a doctor is in an ambulance. And he'd have to be unconscious for that. Go in and say hello."

Daniel sits across from his dad, who doesn't look up from his paper.

"You want the sports section?" He hands it to Daniel.

They both read in companionable silence until she calls them to the table.

Daniel watches her dishing out the food. She looks older than when he last saw her. He does a quick calculation and realizes it must have been a couple of months. Not okay, he tells himself.

"This is great, Mom. You used that paprika you brought back from your trip to Hungary. It makes all the difference."

She smiles, glowing in his praise.

"So how's the job, Daniel?" asks his father.

"It's fine, Dad."

His father is straining to make conversation, and his mother yearns to see them communicate.

"And how much are you making now?"

"I don't know exactly. It pays well."

Will this be the signal to attack? Daniel feels his mother grow tense. He takes another mouthful of food.

"You don't know how much you're earning? What kind of craziness is this? You're asking them to screw you over, aren't you? You're saying, 'Come on, you've got a real sucker here,' aren't you? I've never heard of such a thing." His father looks for support, but his wife concentrates on her plate.

"Dad, they're good people. It's a fair wage."

Daniel uses the hushed tones of this house. His father opens his mouth and then closes it. There are tears in his mother's eyes. Daniel feels his stomach turning but tries to keep eating. A few minutes pass with only the sound of cutlery on plates.

"I just want him to look out for himself, that's all," mutters the father. "I don't want him to get hurt. He's too sensitive. He takes things too hard, instead of understanding that's how the world is and there's nothing anybody can do about it. Is that so terrible? That I don't want my son to get hurt?"

"Of course not," she answers. "Any father would feel the same."

Daniel fights the mounting rage, but again can't control it. "Bullshit, bullshit, bullshit." He speaks in a hoarse whisper. "Stop protecting him. You know what he does to me and you never say anything to stop him."

As usual, his anger is turned on his mother. She pushes her chair away from the table, gets up and goes into the kitchen. The men continue eating, listening to her muffled sniffs.

"She's an optimist," his father says. "Each time she thinks things are going to be better. And she's always disappointed."

"And you don't get disappointed, Dad?"

"No. Not ever."

His mother enters with a Jell-O mould. "You know I can't stand to see my men fighting. Now, Daniel, tell us about the girls in the office. Anybody new?"

"Well, there's one..."

He hears a derisive snort and knows his father understands there will never be a wedding. Nor grandchildren.

"What's her family like?" asks his mother.

Daniel adds some details, then dodges. "Tell me about your trip, Mom."

"It was good to come back to Israel," she says.

This makes his father laugh. "Do you know how much her trips cost? And she's glad to get home."

She takes his teasing. "Europe is beautiful. The people are well-mannered, the streets clean, the scenery magnificent. But it isn't ours. I felt a stranger, even though I had such nice memories from my childhood. Maybe I'm just too old to travel. I'd like you to go visit Budapest though, Daniel. You should see it."

"I'm not interested in seeing the scene of the crimes. You know that," answers Daniel.

His mother gives her husband a sharp glance. He takes the cue. "Your mother and I have been talking."

Daniel sighs.

"And we want to give you a present. We'd like to send you on a tour of Europe. Our treat." The words sound stilted, and he glances at his wife for approval.

"We thought it might be a chance for you to meet some new people," says his mother. "We saw some very nice singles' tours advertised."

They wait for his reaction.

"Thanks for the offer. I'm a little concerned if I'd be able to sleep in a foreign country."

They nod in sympathy.

"Besides, like they say in the ads, there are so many beautiful things to see right here at home. Why travel abroad? You know, if there's extra money, you should go, Dad. Mom doesn't like to travel alone."

His father's breathing gets harsher, a warning signal for the change. "Who has extra money, Daniel? There is no extra money. We were going to do without because your mother is worried about you. She thinks you're depressed. Far too much for a person your age. What do you have to be depressed about anyway?"

"Shhh." His mother puts her hand on her husband's shoulder. "Let him be. Don't fight."

Daniel stands up. "I guess I'll be going now. Thanks for the great dinner."

"But I was going to make coffee," she says.

"Mom, you promised. I have to go now."

She kisses his cheek. "Call me sometimes. A woman likes to be pursued."

"Bye, Dad."

His father is engrossed in muttering and jabbing his fingers into the tablecloth.

His mother sees Daniel to the door.

"Don't take it to heart," she says. "He loves you very much. Try to understand him."

Daniel drives home. He gets undressed quickly and falls into bed. Then he smokes a joint. When no longer conscious, he starts to shiver. At times he retracts part of his body, almost as if he's received a blow, then breaks out in a sweat and wakes to find his pillow drenched.

Chapter 12

Arlene, Mussa and Daniel were always aware of meaning beyond their own experience. Now sometimes they share a supra-emotional pause. None of them sees this as extraordinary or mystical. It's a fact of existence.

The sun is straight overhead on the beach at Ras Burka. They eat their lunch in silence, reassured to be back together after the trip to the gas station. Arlene and Daniel have bought a watermelon from a Bedouin boy and they cut it open and eat it, juice dripping down them into the sand.

The men grab snorkels and masks and run towards the water, Daniel quickly and Mussa slowly, plunging into the ocean.

Arlene enters, feeling the sea wash her in stages. Her friends' heads grow distant. She lies on her back, arms and legs spread for balance, and lets the water buoy her. The sound of the sea is in her ears and the sun touches her. Weightless, she belongs to the ocean.

Above her, the two Egyptian soldiers watch.

"They've left her alone now. *Ya'Allah*, wouldn't I like to go down there and give her what she wants."

"You're lucky it's not Mahmud's shift. If he heard you talking like that, you and your profane thoughts would be buried in the sand."

The other man lights a cigarette. "I'm not afraid of that crazy fanatic. Let him preach his sermons to idiots like himself. You can't even smoke around him without getting your head chewed off. Hand me the binoculars, okay?"

When Arlene swims back to the beach, Daniel and Mussa are nowhere in sight. She covers herself in lotion and takes her book under the palm tree. Charlie, the drummer girl, is caught up in a fantastic web of plots and subplots. Arlene envies her. Where is my contact? she wishes. Why doesn't anyone approach me with a mission? I'm not fulfilled being wife, mother and citizen-by-choice of a unique historical experiment. I need something personally momentous to do. She sighs and opens the book.

Mussa and Daniel swim and watch the coral through their snorkels. It is a universe in itself and they are awed by the vision. The shapes and colours of the undersea mountains and valleys present a strange backdrop for the bizarrely-coloured fish swimming in the ocean's pulsating silence. Each tiny piece of coral with its delicate filigree of holes and fibres is a separate world. As they hold their faces under the surface, they are enclosed with the coral inside the warm salt water.

Between each world is a stretch of clean sand. Daniel and Mussa rest their eyes and minds until their strokes bring them to a new brilliant creation. Finally, they swim shoreward to rest and watch the surface boundary.

They dig holes, piling the loose sand for backrests, and sit in the scooped-out hollows.

"It was a great idea to come here, Daniel."

"You can't imagine what's underneath. You wouldn't even think to look."

"No. I wouldn't have known if you hadn't told me."

The peace between them is a new experience, a mode different from their usual harsh teasing. Daniel isn't sure how to handle it. He watches the water.

Mussa remains dazzled by the contrast between the view of placid ocean and what lies beneath. The surface will never be the same.

"Arlene's all right," says Mussa. "It's okay that she came."

Daniel smiles and they both drift into slumber.

Arlene lets her book drop beside her and stretches her arms above her head, thinking she might nap again. But her mind doesn't want to shut down and she lets it ramble, hoping eventually it will lose power of its own accord. First, she thinks of Yossi and the children. Did Tali go for her orthodontist appointment? How was Maya's arithmetic test? Has Tamir learned any new words? Is Yossi anxious before his big meeting with the client from Germany? They're managing fine, she tells herself. And the family moves out of the foreground of her thoughts.

Daniel and Mussa assume primary focus. Here we are in paradise and we've brought all our city craziness with us. Mussa with his coveting eyes and childlike belief in politics. Daniel, looking for some magic key to explain everything and despairing when the world makes no sense. And me. Not able to define anything at all. The men's images dance inside her.

Now she is alone with the date palm, its branches stirring in the wind. And the longer she focusses on the branches, the sleepier she gets until her mind empties of all conscious thought.

All three nap - daytime sleep, with its own dreams and its own rest patterns. It's a break between activities, a quick foray bounded neither by the preparation rituals of night nor the familiarity of morning. It's sleep that summons them from light to deliver urgent messages.

Arlene dreams she's in a time tunnel. She doesn't know how she recognizes the endless tube as a passageway through time, but she knows it is. She's been walking for a while and she's tired and thirsty. Behind her is a tiny room that was her starting point. Now she's dragging her feet. There is a dusty swirl inside the tube that stings her eyes. She does not know where she is going or how long the journey will take. She follows her feet and trusts there will be an end. Her tongue feels glued to the bottom of her mouth and she keeps prying it up to touch the roof. She began by counting her steps but has given it up as futile.

In front of her it seems to be growing darker. The dust swirls appear whiter against the black as she moves forward. A cold wind is starting to blow but she wonders if the shivering is coming from within her. She turns to look back, but it seems much too far away. And she remembers that she left for an important reason.

She returns to face the dark and keeps walking until she can't see at all and only by stretching her arms to touch the sides of the tube can she give herself enough courage to go on. She wishes she could know if she is moving towards past or future.

The line ''Just Whistle a Happy Tune'' plays in her head. She laughs. Then the sides of the passage disappear and she stops laughing. She doesn't know if she is inside the passage or has come out. Everything is dark.

Arlene moves to the right, hoping to hit the side of the tube. She doesn't. She is bounded by nothing. Frantically, she searches for the tunnel's exit but it is nowhere to be found. She closes her eyes and not moving, creates her own darkness. She feels safe. Then she hears the whispers.

''Arlene... Arlene...''

Out of the dark void someone has recognized her. She is not alone in the blackness.

''This way,'' the voices say.

She follows the whispers. She tries talking, though she doesn't feel sound coming from her lips.

''Where am I?''

''This way,'' they say.

The darkness begins to warm. She knows she is in time past. ''You've made a mistake. I'm not Arlene. Please,'' she says, ''don't call me Arlene.''

''This way.''

She sits down, but the ground bumps her along like a ride at an amusement park. And it's getting hotter and hotter. She lies down, but she's on a bed of jelly that can't be grasped. The pulsating force that pushes her is growing stronger. She wants to scream but her mouth is so dry it comes out as a croak. The whispers have stopped. She lets her body go loose and be pulled along to what she now knows is the fire where she will be burned, destroyed and lose all memory. She will return to her life - and wakes up crying, not remembering why.

Mussa dreams he is beating olive branches with a stick to shake the fruit onto the ground. But no matter how hard he hits them, the olives refuse to fall. The harder he beats the tree, the more his rage grows and his shoulder and back muscles strain as he whips. In the distance he hears his mother calling the family to dinner but pays no attention. It's as if he is attached to his stick with no choice but to function until released. The green olives laugh at him and there is nothing he can do.

There is one olive, wrinkled and spoiled, that if it were to fall would be left on the ground. This olive puckers its skin and makes itself even more shrivelled in order to drive him crazy. But hard as he smacks the branches, the olives will not fall. Mussa's body is lathered in sweat and his tongue hangs from his mouth. The hand that holds the stick is starting to bleed.

He feels the touch of his little sister and his arm falls to his side. He is exhausted,

"Mama wants us to come eat now."

Mussa follows the girl, trailing the stick behind him. They walk through the grove, stepping on the olives that others have shaken from the trees. He feels shame at his defeat. He watches his sister's bare feet stepping in front of him. They seem unattached to the sturdy brown legs above them. After they've been walking for a long time, Mussa raises his head and drops his stick. The landscape before him is unfamiliar.

"Where are we?" he asks.

"We're on our way home for supper," his sister answers. "The food is on the table." She keeps moving forward.

"But this isn't the way home," says Mussa.

"You just don't remember."

Mussa follows the child in silence. He rubs his sore shoulder and thinks about the meal waiting for him. They don't seem to be getting any closer. The girl's feet hardly touch the ground as she increases her pace.

"I can't keep up with you," he calls.

"You're getting too old, Mussa. Too set in your ways. You better hurry or Mama won't wait for you."

He begins to run and finds it much easier than he had thought. He's able to keep pace with his sister. She takes his hand and they move over the ground together.

They enter a mountainous area. They are in a *wadi* cut deep between earth mounds. The mounds are so high he can't see the top. They run along the dry river bed through small green vegetation. A trickle of water sometimes appears above ground to wet their toes. Mussa feels no strain in running. His fatigue disappears and he is light and full of energy. He laughs out loud and his sister joins him.

Soon they are moving without touching the ground. Below them the river has started to flow. They soar above it, following its course as it winds through the dried land.

"Are you having fun, Mussa?" asks his sister.

"I could go on like this forever."

The girl nods in satisfaction. "This is a shortcut. I always go home this way."

"Who else have you told?" he asks.

"You're the first."

The river pulses stronger beneath them and Mussa feels himself dropping into a large pool. He lets himself sink into the cool water, then surfaces and shakes his curls in the sun. His sister is perched on an overhanging rock, smiling at him.

"I don't think you're bringing me to Mama," he says.

"Of course I am. Mama's right here."

Mussa looks around and doesn't see anybody. And when he turns back to question his sister, she is gone. He starts swimming back and forth, easing out his sore shoulder and waiting for the child to return. He hears Daniel call him.

"I was swimming in the bottom of a *wadi*," he says.

Daniel dreamed he was inside his bottle of tears that the neighbour gave him when he was small. His tiny form was surrounded by tinted green glass. The bottle was placed on a free-standing pedestal. He could see outside and hear sounds, while he stayed corked and protected within. He could breathe both the air at the neck of the bottle and submerged in the liquid.

He was in a large, windowless room with a door in every wall. The walls stretched high but the cork prevented Daniel from seeing the ceiling. He found that by crying he could sink further into the tears. By expelling air from his mouth in a slow hiss, he would rise towards the cork.

Plunging and floating, he became aware of two figures that entered from one of the doors. They were dressed in royal robes, crimson-coloured and trimmed with ermine. Their crowned heads, twinkling with jewels, were bent in earnest conversation. At first Daniel could not hear the words, but he found that by staying inside the tear-water with his ear pressed to the side of the glass bottle, he could understand everything.

"This world must end, you know," said the king.

"But it does seem a pity," the queen answered.

"If you want to back out, you better make up your mind. I don't want to be left holding the bag when it's over and you complaining it was all my fault."

"Can't I be sad and still hold to my decision?" She moved away from the king.

"Do you want us to end up in that bottle like Daniel, drowning in our own tears?"

Daniel tried to protest that he wasn't drowning, that now he could breathe in water. But the two figures outside the bottle couldn't hear him.

"If all you're going to do is cry about it," the king went on, "then let's forget the whole thing."

The queen composed herself. "I cry too much as it is. I don't believe in slow death and prolonged agony. I've given up hope for miracle cures. I'll stick by our decision."

The king and queen embraced and made their exit. Daniel wished he could have gone with them and felt for the first time a glimmer of regret at being in the bottle. Then there was a stirring from another doorway and he turned to see a figure resembling his father but taller and draped in a grey hooded cloak. The figure approached the bottle and pressed his face against the glass. It was distorted, nose pressed flat, eyes bulging and mouth leaving clouds of steam. The giant lips moved at Daniel, who had retreated to the far side of the glass wall.

"Daniel, it's up to you," the mouth pushed the sound at him. "You heard them, didn't you? So what are you going to do about it?"

A giant ear pressed its folds to the bottle.

"I'm not the right person for the job," Daniel answered. "Sorry. Get someone else, okay?"

The ear waited, listening for more. Daniel blew a few air bubbles at it through the water.

"Go away, please. I'm not the person you want me to be. I'd like to save the world but I can't."

The big ear began to cry. Tears dripped from its hole and spilled down the lobe. Daniel stared at it until he felt a cool wind that woke him up.

"I dreamt about water too," he tells Mussa.

Mussa gets up. "Let's walk back. I'm so water-logged I can't take any more."

They start for the campsite, brushing the sand off their bodies. The sun is beginning to set and their shadows reach into the water, parts of themselves yearning for the coral world. They walk in silence, not sure of where they've been, trying to grasp the fading memory of their visions. Neither can shake the feeling of not sharing the same time zone. The other seems more like part of the landscape than a companion. When they see their bottled candle burning in the dusk ahead of them, they quicken their pace, and sharing the homecoming, feel closer.

"Welcome back!" Arlene smiles as she puts her book down. "I was getting worried."

Daniel and Mussa go to the tent to change into jeans and shirts.

"I'll make coffee," she calls.

They sit around the light, Mussa and Daniel quenching their thirst from the water bottle and Arlene supervising the small pot of Turkish coffee as it boils, cools, and boils again. Arlene is as distanced by her nap as the men are. After she woke, she found herself reading the same sentences over and over, unable to concentrate on her book. The last time she can remember having this sensation was when Tamir was born. The hospital kept him an extra day and she had gone home alone. She lived those hours with no identity, looking at the world as if she were the newborn. It was a day she stored in a vault so deep she'd forgotten it was there.

The three sip coffee. Then she lies stretched on her blanket, watching the stars come out. Mussa sits hunched over the bottle and its flickering candle. Daniel looks towards the black water. Small bugs chirp and whir. Later, Daniel brings out hard salami, pickles and pita. Mussa makes a driftwood fire. There is no conversation. A three-quarter moon shines down as they eat.

After the meal, Mussa stands. "I'm going in. You coming?" And he undresses.

Daniel follows him, and then Arlene. The water warms and caresses their naked bodies and they glitter in the moonlight. The three swim separately, leave the water, quickly towel themselves dry and dress. No one speaks.

Mahmud is back on shift. He is nauseated and feels his head is about to explode in a paroxysm of rage. His body shivers, despite his woollen uniform. I can't take this anymore, he thinks. Why am I being subjected to this? I shouldn't have to look at this filth.

Unless there is a reason. Unless it is the Will of Allah that I am here to witness.

Mahmud is filled with understanding.

But of course! That must be true. I am to be His Servant. I am to disobey man-made military orders and perform His Greater Will.

The imagined flight of obedience sends him into further shivering.

Chapter 13

The difference between the three on the beach and the man at his army post is one of balance - between inner and outer selves. Mahmud is on duty, protecting enemies who threaten his cosmic order. He cannot be at peace in this paradox. The two men and the woman feel the sand and sea within them and are in harmony.

In the morning as Arlene, Daniel and Mussa clean up their breakfast things, two cars pull down onto their stretch of sand. As the three watch the approach of the beige Ford Escort and the white Saab, both with Israeli licence plates, they feel outraged at the intrusion.

"We knew paradise couldn't last forever. One day we were going to get kicked out of here," comments Arlene.

"Maybe it's a sign," adds Mussa. "We've about reached the peak anyway. Maybe it's time to head back."

"Or move on to someplace else," says Daniel. "I'm not ready for Tel Aviv. Actually, I'm not sure I'll ever be ready for the city."

The cars stop at the other end of the beach, keeping their distance from the original settlers. The doors open.

"Oh, no," cries Daniel. "They've got kids."

There are five children and they spill out onto the sand with whoops of relief, flinging their shorts and T-shirts aside and sprinting for the water. They shout to each other in Hebrew.

"You guys want me to go scare them off?" offers Mussa. "I can do my Arab militant number and mention my connection with the guards up there. And I'll say you two are my Palestinian cousins visiting from Los Angeles."

"Go ahead, Mussa. Make my day," says Arlene.

Daniel listens to his friends and is glad of this trust. "Well, I think we should go over and say hello to them and break the tension," he says. "Then each can be in his own territory and respect the distance."

"Daniel, you have voiced my political sentiments," says Mussa.

They walk slowly towards the group setting up a large tent with plastic windows. The two couples work together in familiar companionship. They pause as the three approach.

"Hi," says the woman with short blond hair. "Sorry if we're spoiling your solitude, but this is our favourite camping place too. It's our third year here."

One of the men comes forward with outstretched hand. He reaches Mussa first. "My name's Avner."

"Mussa." The hand holds his firmly, even though Mussa is primed for the slightest hesitation when the Jew hears the Arab name.

The rest of the adult introductions are made - Adi, Shula, Noam.

"We'll leave you to your settling in," says Arlene.

They walk back to their site.

"They don't seem the rude and littering kind," says Daniel, looking for ways to overcome the invasion.

Arlene is certain the woman, Shula, has appraised her relationship to the two men. Only now does she feel shame at last night's swim, imagining how her own children would have seen it. Mussa senses this and puts his arm lightly around her.

"These people are okay," he says. "They'll let us be."

He notices Daniel walking with a forlorn expression and puts his arm around him too. "Come on, you two. I'm an expert at this stuff. I know when the second dialogue is going on, when what they say to your face has nothing to do with what's going on inside. This group is all right. Trust me."

"It isn't the same though, is it?" says Arlene.

"No, it isn't," answers Daniel, and Mussa nods. "But it's going to be okay. It's still not Tel Aviv and we're still on vacation. We can ignore them just like we ignore those guys in the guardhouse. They're part of the scenery. Charming and quaint, reminding us we're in a geographical place - a fixed point - and not floating anchorless in the universe."

"All right, all right. You've convinced me." Arlene remembers Daniel persuading her to come on the trip. "But they make me remember we're not here forever."

Mussa pulls them both to him and they stop walking to form a tight embrace. They stand, eyes closed, feet planted in the sand and the sea breeze on their backs. They can hear each other's breathing as it grows heavier and their bodies vibrate to faster tempos. A powerful battery is being charged. Arlene is the first to feel her knees give way and she sinks into the sand. The men let go and squat to sit beside her. All three are flushed and panting. They stare at the sea.

"What are we going to do?" Daniel breaks the silence.

"Nothing," Arlene is quick to answer. "Absolutely nothing."

Mussa laughs and he and Daniel share a look of disbelief at the woman's words. Something has already been done.

"Daniel, come on. Let's you and I go for a drive in the van. I need to get off the beach for a while," says Mussa. He stands and brushes the sand from his shorts. "Are you coming?"

Daniel looks at Arlene, who still gazes at the sea. And as he walks with Mussa towards the van, Daniel shivers at a sudden realization. It's as if he's been deaf his whole life and suddenly hears sound. Years of others describing it to him and his own anger at his incapacity to grasp meaning. But now he gets it - what those others called love. He begins to laugh. An unchoked laugh. A laugh he's never known.

Mussa has never heard this sound either. "What's going on, man? You lost your mind completely?"

Daniel can't stop laughing and Mussa soon joins him. Daniel's giggles subside, and by the time he turns the key in the ignition he can talk.

"You want a cigarette, Mussa? I've got extra packs under the dashboard. Light me one too." He directs the van onto the highway and they head south. As he smokes Daniel calms down. "I feel better leaving her alone there now that the other campers are around. There are advantages to civilization."

Mussa looks ahead, concentrating on the cigarette, knowing that his friend will say more. The road spins out before them, hugging the ocean's curve, while the protective mountains seem to be following from behind.

Daniel gathers his thoughts. "Something important happened on the beach. I'm not talking about the three of us. Right now I'm telling you about me." He passes a slow-moving truck. "People have tried to educate me about what's going on between people. You, for example, kept pounding on me about how an Arab kid looks at the world. I understood on an intellectual level, but it wasn't inside. Ten minutes ago all that changed. That's why I couldn't stop laughing."

Mussa shakes his head. "Daniel, sweet Daniel, how you got from those sparks when we were all touching there to little kids who are turning out crazier than we are, I don't know. I'm telling you that you'll never know what it's like for those kids, no matter how hard I try to get the idea across. You have to grow up in it. You have to be an Arab."

Daniel starts laughing again, slapping the edge of the driver's wheel.

"Man, you are stranger than usual. Did you smoke this morning?"

"Mussa, I'm happy."

"Good. Very good," Mussa says, and adds in Yiddish, "May you be protected from the evil eye."

Daniel laughs so hard he has to pull onto the shoulder.

Mussa quietly finishes his cigarette. When he's done, he opens the door. "Move over. I'll drive." He gets in the other side and pulls them back onto the road.

They move on with occasional snorts as Daniel tries to relax.

"See, Mussa, it doesn't matter what you say. I just sit here and listen and it makes perfect sense. It's as if I were you and I was talking to myself. There are no contradictions, everything fits. God, I feel good. I've always wanted to know what people mean when they say that. Sort of a released feeling?"

"Sure, Daniel. That and no pain and being glad you're alive."

Daniel sighs. "What a waste to have missed out on this."

"You're just turned on by the girl." Mussa keeps his eyes on the road. "Haven't you ever felt turned on before?"

"That's it, Mussa. I'm in love."

"Yeah, love."

Mussa lets the van speed down the road hardly touching the wheel on the straight surface. He is enjoying Daniel and letting the euphoria relieve the tension from the beach. "You're all right, Daniel. When we drive the Jews into the sea, I'll get you a ticket to Switzerland."

Daniel closes his eyes, letting the rhythm of the wheels engulf him. He feels Mussa handing him a cigarette and takes it without looking. It's important to sort out what's happening and the thoughts race through him. I've grown up not knowing something essential about life. But today there's a change. I've lost control. Like I do when I'm fucking. Anything can happen to me now.

His head feels like exploding. "Let's stop for a swim. I've got to cool down. Pull into Nuweiba. We can buy a cold drink."

There are campers all over the popular beach and dozens of half-naked girls, who look up enticingly.

"Wow," Mussa whispers as they make their way to the kiosk. "Are you thinking what I'm thinking about how to cool down? These tall, blond Scandinavian women are crazy for us Mediterranean types. Look at them."

"I'm looking," answers Daniel.

They sip beer under the striped awning of the kiosk.

One of the girls pulls on a T-shirt. She rises and Mussa and Daniel realize she's making her way towards them. Her girlfriend waits more demurely on her beach towel.

"What are we going to do?" Mussa nudges his companion.

"If you're asking me for advice, then we're really in trouble."

"Hi, guys," she says in English. She has a lilting accent. "You're new on the beach. I'm Kristen and over there is my friend Linda. You will join us?"

"Sure. Why not? I'm Mussa. And this is my friend Daniel."

"You are an Arab?" She has made her choice.

Mussa nods assent.

"Come, Daniel," she says. "You will like Linda very much."

Kristen pulls off her T-shirt when she reaches her towel, making introductions. Mussa and Daniel sit on the sand, clutching their beer cans.

"You are both Israelis?" Linda asks.

"I'm Palestinian. He's Israeli," says Mussa.

"But you both live in Israel," Linda persists. "I was there for a few months. On a kibbutz. There were Arabs too. Working there from the nearby village. I like Israelis."

"You mean Israelis and Palestinians," Kristen corrects as she winks at Mussa.

As he listens to the chit-chat, Daniel feels the old panic rising inside him. "I'm sorry," he says, "we have to go." He gets up.

Mussa shakes his head. "Please excuse my friend, ladies. He's not feeling well. Too much sun."

Back in the van, they head north to their campsite.

"I'm sorry I acted so crazy, Mussa, but we were right to leave. We need to get back to her."

Mussa's thoughts are complicated. He doesn't trust himself to answer Daniel. The uppermost feeling is fear and this surprises him.

What am I afraid of? I feel no jealousy towards Daniel. I'm excited by Arlene. And the logistics of a threesome don't bother me either. But I feel like I'm about to lose something, to give it away. What am I so frightened of losing?

He turns on the radio.

"Hey, do we need this noise? Gives me a headache."

"It's a ballad in Arabic. About a strange young man who wanders into a village and steals a bride from her wedding bed."

Back at the beach, Arlene doesn't hear them until they are standing by her towel and she feels their shadows on her back. Shading her eyes, she looks up.

"I'm glad you're here. The book was getting my head all fucked up. I was in a refugee camp in Lebanon, getting bombed in an Israeli reprisal raid."

Mussa nods. "I've visited some camps in Gaza. Talked to people there. When we get back, I can take you. You can talk to them in English. You should learn what's going on."

"But you must stay by me."

"I will, Arlene."

It is the first time he has called her by name. She starts to cry. The men sit down on either side of her.

"I was also thinking about my grandmother," she says. "She was a refugee from Russia who fled with her family to America."

Mussa and Daniel look at the water as she talks.

"I loved her very much. Her mother died when she was ten, leaving my grandmother to raise her brothers. Her father was gone all day, working in a factory. She went to grammar school when she could and finished high school at night after she was a mother herself. She married at sixteen. Her husband was a good provider and they lived comfortably. After the kids were grown, she could have relaxed, played bridge like her friends. But she didn't. Grandma got involved in politics."

She checks to see if the men are listening.

"She organized rallies and raised money for Israel and she campaigned for the American Democratic Party. Sometimes Grandpa and her would have terrible arguments about the amount of time she was devoting to her 'causes,' but she wouldn't stop.

"I only knew Grandma through visits, but she gave me whatever sense I have of meaning in life. She always talked to me as if I was an adult. She read everything I wrote. She was so proud of me when I moved to Israel.

"In her letters to me she tried to hide the growing bitterness inside her. All her hopes for the New World that had promised so much were being crushed. It was cracking at the seams. She had a close friend who was beaten to death in her own parking garage. She read in the papers about racial and sexual violence. And this reminded her of Hitler. She wrote about that. The damage he did was not only to the millions who died. Hitler betrayed her belief in what it was to be human. Grandma spent her life trying to reinstate that belief, doing what she could to change things for the better. She always said I had to do this too.

"But in the end she felt defeated.

"My mother visited her in the hospital the day she died. Do you know what she said? 'How did I get involved in this war anyway?' And all the time I feel like I've got to prove her fight was worth it."

She pauses.

"Neither of you can really see me - not you, Mussa, whose people think they own the present world rights to suffering, nor you, Daniel, whose family tragedy cut you off from so much. I also have a history and connections. My heritage is as old as yours and I've got my own obligations."

The tension of the morning is back. Nobody speaks. Mussa and Daniel still watch the sea. Arlene picks up her book, but it is impossible to read so she too sits and stares at the water.

"Well, this is the way I see it," Daniel says. "We can sit here glued to the sand until the tide washes over us, or we can get on with it. I'm for getting on with it."

Daniel stands and reaches for their hands. "Come on. We'll go to the tent and smoke and talk a little. This may be the first time in my life I'm sure I'm doing the right thing."

But in the tent there doesn't seem to be any need for talk. They close the flaps, leaving a small opening for air, and sit cross-legged and knees touching to smoke until they are all smiling.

Arlene stands first and peels off her suit. The men undress, and they all hold and touch. There is no shyness, nothing new to discover. They come and go inside each other and their skins grow slick and glisten. Sometimes one shudders and writhes while the other two cling and comfort. Sometimes it is two while the third pets them both. And when it is three, they explode in laughter.

Eventually, they separate, and each lies staring wide-eyed into nothing, alone again within their own skin.

The first sounds that penetrate are those of the children shouting in the distance.

"After this, there is only remembering," says Arlene.

Chapter 14

Mussa wakes first, dresses and starts the fire. The smell of coffee reaches the two others and they dress and join him. The sun is setting and there is a chill in the air. In the purple light the mountains seem larger than usual. A slight wind blows the smoke towards Daniel and he moves between his friends, closing the gap. They stare into the flames, listening to the crackling wood and the lapping sea.

The other campers also have a fire, and that glow reaches them too. The children are at last quiet.

Above them, Mahmud reports for duty. He has a double shift to get an extra day on the weekend. His wife has just given birth to their first son and he wants to be home for the relatives who will be coming from miles around. He is already tired as he comes on duty after two sleepless nights disturbed by the colicky baby. He hopes he will not have to soil himself with the sight of the lewd infidels.

"There are more of them down there," says a soldier who is leaving. "Children too. I don't understand why they don't use their own beaches. Why do they have to come here?"

"It's an act of aggression." Mahmud's voice is irritable, tired of explaining. "They come to stake out territory."

"Maybe they just like the beach here," says the soldier who has come on duty with Mahmud.

"Don't argue with Mahmud. He has all the right responses and anything you say will be wrong."

Mahmud turns to confront the one who has teased him, but the soldier jumps into the waiting jeep with the others and is gone. The two men on night shift heat tea on the kerosene burner and settle into their routine. Mahmud prepares himself for a long night's educational marathon.

"Well, I'm hungry." Arlene heads for the van. "I think there are some cans of meatballs left. I'll warm them up. You guys should find some wood."

The men scout for driftwood and talk. They eat the mush in tomato sauce that she has heated, then build the fire for warmth.

"Arlene," Daniel says, "Mussa and I think it's a good idea to get going now. We could reach Eilat by morning. If you want, you can buy something there for your kids."

"No," she answers quickly.

The men look at her.

"I don't want to stop." Her voice is abrupt. "If we're leaving, then let's drive right through like we did coming here. Let's rinse the dishes, pack the stuff and get on the road." She starts to stand up.

"Hold on, kid." Mussa's voice is sharp and stops her. "What's going on? You sit right there until we straighten this out. What's up?"

"You two are something else. You don't have a clue how your announcement sounds to me, do you?"

They look baffled. Given another minute, Arlene knows she'll feel sorry for them. She works to hold onto her anger.

"You're pushing me out again. Making a decision to bring us to an end, sending me back to be a mother."

Daniel is quick to try and soothe her. "Mussa and I want to protect you, Arlene. We think you're in over your head and it's time we got you back to where you belong. This is some crazy fantasy that's happening here and we don't want you to get hurt."

She can find nothing to say.

"You should trust us by now, Arlene," adds Mussa. "Daniel and I were talking about how beautiful you are and how fine it would be if all of us could be together forever. And, of course, how impossible that is. So we better get you home to your family before it's too late."

"But why late for me? What about you? Doesn't this mean as much to you?" Her voice is soft.

"Of course it does," says Daniel. "For me more than anybody. I've never known what closeness was until now. But you have the most to lose."

She shakes her head in disappointment. The fire lights their faces, catching eyes still glowing from within. Mussa makes coffee and in the silence they can hear the families at the other end of the beach singing campfire songs. Daniel reaches out to touch her hand but she withdraws it.

"So, Daniel," says Mussa. "Maybe we are wrong to try and protect her. She wants to be out there suffering with the rest of us."

If we could stay here in this place, thinks Daniel. We could wander for forty years. Just the three of us. Let the rest of the world blow itself up.

"It doesn't help to add another martyr to the pyre," Daniel says.

"Goddammit!" Arlene finds her voice. "I'm not looking for a way to feel terrible. I'd like my life to be one long love-making session, but that's not going to be. Just stop putting me out on the periphery. Don't hide behind protecting me, so you don't have to deal with how frightened you are. None of us knows what's going to happen after we get back. And if imagining me in my routine brings you comfort, forget it! You'll have to find other means of pacifying yourselves."

"Fine," Mussa answers for both of them.

They watch the fire.

"We're all a result of our past," Mussa continues, lighting a cigarette and inhaling deeply. "It's not our fault. Knowing that has made my life easier. It's the only way I know how to function. And it's the only way to deal with the present.

Like your grandmother brought her Jewish beliefs with her to America, Arlene. As you've brought your American beliefs here. Yes, even now I see you as an American."

She listens quietly.

"I'm sitting here," continues Mussa, "with two Jews, feeling closer to them than I have to any human being. We've completed a ritual mating that would be seen by the world as corrupt. I know this isn't true. I know what's going on between us is beyond Jew and Arab, beyond male and female."

His voice breaks.

Arlene and Daniel sit in respectful silence while their friend keens in mourning. The fire burns low. Arlene opens her arms and Mussa lets himself be held.

"I've cried before, you know," Mussa says as a challenge, and his friends smile. He lowers his eyes and drinks his coffee. Daniel lights a cigarette. There is only the sound of the fire. The campers down the beach have long since retired. Mahmud and his companion are dozing.

"You know," Daniel says, "when I look at you two I don't feel so loathsome. I don't want to die. And I even think there may be beauty in the world."

He feels their minds drifting away from him.

Chapter 15

Arlene, Daniel and Mussa swim in the waning starlight and then dress. They gather their things on the sand and take down the tent and awning. As they pack, dawn is breaking over the sea and they turn to stand still and breathe its beauty.

Daniel climbs in the driver's side. Arlene is next to him, and Mussa sits behind them with an arm around each. With a last glance at the beach, Daniel starts the motor and they pull up the road to the highway. He drives quickly towards the border.

Mahmud breathes a sigh of relief. The other soldier is asleep, so Mahmud's curse goes unheard. He is very tired and the wool uniform is agonizing against his skin. As the sun grows hotter, the rash on his thighs begins to throb.

The two families on the beach waken. The children are the first to tumble out of the tent flap and run for the water. The parents follow sleepily to start their morning coffee. The oldest child, Boaz, approaches his mother.

"Those other people have left, Mom. Can we go over and roll down the hill?"

She shades her eyes to look at the gleaming white spill of sand where the children played last year and the year before. "Don't be too long, Boaz. We're making breakfast."

The boy shouts to the others and they gallop down the beach. The mother watches, smiling.

Boaz slows his pace and lets the smaller children overtake him. His sister looks back, laughing as she passes. When they reach the shining hill and begin their ascent, they slow their pace.

What's going on there? Mahmud asks himself. What do they think they're doing? He squints, then reaches for the binoculars. It's the children. That's the plan then. The van must have brought weapons for these others and they've sent the children to put us off guard. And when they reach the top, they'll throw the grenades and roll down.

Mahmud threads the bullets into the machine gun quietly so as not to wake the other soldier. I can handle this, he thinks. With the help of Allah.

The little girl stops to catch her breath and looks towards the top of the hill. "Hey," she calls down, "I can see the guardhouse. And a soldier." She waves at the figure.

The others look where she is pointing.

"First one up to the flag wins," says Boaz. He takes off, waving his arms and shouting, "Forward! To the top, comrades!" The children follow, laughing.

Mahmud counts to one hundred, making sure he has all five in range before he starts firing. It is only a matter of seconds before the bodies lie still, larger ones flung on the smaller.

The parents hear the shots and see no movement on the white hill. They begin running and as they approach, they can hear their children's moans.

The other soldier has awakened and he throws himself on Mahmud, pulling the gun away from him. He grabs the binoculars. "Mahmud, what have you done? They're children. *Ya'Allah*, what are we going to do?"

Mahmud lies on the ground confused. "Quickly! Give me the gun! The adults are right behind them! Call for help!"

The soldier in command is frightened and screams at the two couples through a bullhorn. "Do not approach until the investigator comes from headquarters."

A spray of bullets sweeps the beach.
The parents watch their dying children.

The van speeds down the highway and reaches the border. The Egyptians wave the threesome through the metal barrier after a glance at their passports. The Israelis ask them to get out and usher them into an office in a wooden shed.

The soldier's face across the desk is lined with worry. He looks at the two men and the woman in front of him, their passports in his hand, and addresses Daniel. "You have been camping in the Sinai. Where?"

"Ras Burka."

"When did you leave?"

"Sunrise."

"What's going on? The Egyptians have blocked off the road."

"A couple of families are camping there. That's all."

The soldier looks at Arlene and Mussa. "You didn't notice anything unusual?"

"Nothing," they answer.

The officer hands them their passports. "All right then," he says. "Welcome home."

Acknowledgements

I thank my friend and mentor for her guidance and support. I thank my family, Alan, Sarah and Beni, for their patience and love.

Lisa Herman

(photo by Alan Kanter)